Other Titles By
Katherine D. Jones

CUFFED BY CANDLELIGHT: AN EROTIC ANTHOLOGY

DEEP DOWN

LOVE WORTH FIGHTING FOR

UNDERCOVER LOVER

WORTH THE WAIT

Dangerous Dilemmas

Katherine D. Jones

Parker Publishing, LLC

Noire Passion is an imprint of Parker Publishing, LLC.

Copyright © 2007 by Katherine D. Jones

Published by Parker Publishing, LLC
P.O. Box 380-844
Brooklyn, NY 11238
www.parker-publishing.com

ISBN 13: 978-1-60043-014-5

First Edition

Manufactured in the United States of America

Dedication

To readers who like a little spice, a little suspense and a lot of romance!
I'm willing to keep this thang going if you are—
keep reading and I'll keep writing.

Acknowledgements

I have to thank the wonderful folks at Parker Publishing for this experience and the opportunity to write hot, edgy stories for my readers.

A million thanks to Deatri King-Bey, who we should probably canonize for dealing with me—and my drama.

A big thank you to my girls, Angie Daniels, Maureen Smith, Shelia Goss, Gwyneth Bolton, Karen White-Owens and Nathasha Brooks-Harris. Y'all make it fun!

This has been a terrific learning and growth experience during the short time we've worked together. I appreciate your faith and guidance from the bottom of my heart.

Also, I owe a debt of gratitude to the readers who continue to support me, my family near and far and my friends—you guys are awesome! As my youngest son would say.

To my 'I' boys—thanks a million! Love you guys.

CHAPTER ONE

4:00 A.M.

Kayla stole a glance at the clock, as if peeking at it would make time slow down enough to allow her another couple of hours of rest. Kayla breath out heavily. If she didn't get up soon, she would be late to open the restaurant. "Why, why, why," she complained to the empty space of the room. Five minutes later, she rolled out of the bed to make her way to the bathroom.

The water from the shower was hot enough to fog up the mirror, but she ignored the fact that she would be like a prune once she finally came out from under the spray. Right now, all she thought about was how much she needed the heat.

Water sluiced down her back, massaging the kinks out of tight muscles. She exhaled slowly. It would be nice to have a pair of male hands to rub out the tension. Hell, forget the tension, it would be nice to have the comfort of a pair of male hands *period*! A wry smile crept along her lips. There was one particular restaurant patron Kayla imagined would fit the bill...perfectly.

She and Tracey, her assistant manager, jokingly referred to him as *Mr. Special*. No matter what else was on the menu, he ordered the daily lunch special, no fuss, no substitutions.

Kayla had begun to make it a point to be at the front counter or circulating among the crowd every day around 12:30 P.M. You could set your watch by him, but time was the least of what she thought about when he was around.

Body delicious was his second nickname. But that was her own *personal* pet name for him. From what she had been able to gather without a formal introduction, his name was Cole. She'd heard him on his cell phone plenty of times while she walked around to make sure her customers were happy.

The mere thought of him made her lick her lips. He embodied the term *fine as hell.* Wavy brown hair, a thin mustache, sculpted goatee and amber-flecked brown eyes for starters. Broad shoulders, a narrow waist and long legs finished the handsome package.

But after watching him come into the restaurant on a regular basis, Kayla wanted to do more than share an occasional greeting. Images of his sexy, thick lips and muscular body seemed to invade her consciousness at the most inopportune times. For instance, there was nothing like imagining a kiss sensual and passionate enough to buckle her knees while making the bank deposits.

Kayla chuckled. *If you only knew what you do to me.* On some level, she felt she should be ashamed of her scandalous thoughts, but somehow she wasn't. It just made seeing him when he came in that much more exciting. As it stood already, he could set her body aflame from simple eye contact.

Cole was an all day *contact* high. Sort of like she felt after watching the actor Frankie G—and she didn't give a damn what role he played, just as long as she was treated to the visual treat of seeing him. *Ummm…Hmmm…*there was fine and then there was *you gonna make me wet myself* fine. Kayla licked her lips again as if tasting him. Yeah, Cole was all that…especially in her dreams, which he invaded nightly.

Most times, in the middle of the night, she ended up soaked with sweat, moisture pooled between her legs. In the latest installment of her fantasy with Cole, they shared a quiet evening at home, eating the delectable dinner they prepared together. She enjoyed the sight of a man working it in the kitchen. Cooking showed off one's passion…one's zeal for life. Dinner was just the beginning because the real fun started with *dessert—champagne and strawberries and cream.*

Ice wine and slow, hypnotic kisses began the next course. Cole rubbed the sweet succulent fruit against her lips, already kissed to fullness then dipped in again for another taste. His hungry mouth devoured hers, letting her know how much he wanted her. After kissing her

2

soundly, he moved his lips down her neck, blazing a trail of heat over her entire body. Cole *decorated* her with the strawberries and cream and nibbled off every inch of delectable juice. Then he moved his mouth lower...and lower...until he reached her quivering feminine core, which begged for his attention.

As he ate her out, she could feel the gentle, insistent pressure of his mouth against her lower lips. Kayla's breathing came out in short desperate gasps as she imagined Cole burying his tongue deep inside of her, drawing out her nectar, taking her to new heights of ecstasy. He was patient, well-practiced and damned good.

Kayla trembled as her hands rubbed the throbbing bud between her legs. Working it back and forth and up and down until she felt the first stirrings of orgasm. A few minutes later, her entire body shook in a powerful climax.

After thinking about him, she often found herself pulsating with need and desire—and today was no different. Kayla moaned aloud. *Damn*, she wanted to feel the real Cole next to her.

Leaning against the back wall of the tumbled marble shower stall, she waited for the feelings to subside. At this rate, she would never make it to work. She turned off the water then grabbed a thick towel off the door hook. She chastised herself for even allowing her mind to go there. There was no use in thinking about what would *not* be.

Cole, whatever his last name was, would have to continue to be a fantasy because her reality did not allow the time or inclination to maintain a relationship. Instead, her romantic life would have to remain relegated to rich fantasy and fairytale dates. *And lots of hand jobs...*

Fool me once, shame on you; fool me twice, shame on me. Her ex-lover, David, was gone, and she certainly didn't want the kind of drama romantic involvements brought. Not for a long time...

Kayla shook off thoughts of both Cole and David as she quickly dressed, her focus once again on the business at hand. She couldn't afford to be selfish, not when she had other people who depended on her. Her needs had to take a back seat to the legacy of her parents. As an only child, she'd learned early on about responsibility and sacrifice.

Dangerous Dilemmas

Anke and James had been loving and affectionate parents, if not strict and goal oriented. Kayla had always known the path her life would take, had always known she would someday take over the restaurant. And maybe she had always assumed that Mr. Wonderful would show up one day to help her with the family business, probably without her having to look too hard for him.

Marriage, in her opinion, was less about love and more about necessity. She admired what her parents had shared for forty years, but this was a new day. Kayla no longer believed in the fairytale of love and romance. She just needed a working relationship with someone she could tolerate every now and again.

Kayla brushed her shoulder-length hair out if its wrap, added lip gloss with just a hint of red to her full mouth and was ready to walk out the door.

Cole was a good fantasy, but that was about the extent of it. Daily, she told herself she wasn't ready for another relationship. It became her mantra whenever she felt the stab of loneliness pierce through her heart. Lately, the pep talks had become more frequent.

Whew! Kayla paused at the front door with her hand on the knob. Thoroughly talked out of the desire to pursue a relationship, now, she was ready for work. Another quick glance at the clock in her foyer. *Not bad.* She still had twenty minutes to make it down Highway 46 to the restaurant.

It was 5:00 A.M. by the time she parked in her space. The red and white sign read, *Williams Family Diner.* She stopped momentarily to read it, for what had to be the one-millionth time since she'd learned to read at four years of age. A slight shiver ran down her spine as the wind rustled in the predawn hours of the morning. She looked toward the sky. *Are you guys trying to tell me something?*

4

This was a positively ungodly hour to be at work, but for the past twenty-seven years, this was the only life she'd ever known. Her parents had passed away three years ago in a freak car accident, but Kayla could swear she still felt their spirits as she moved around the restaurant and its grounds.

Which brought about a disturbing thought—was it them or was it guilt? Kayla hoped they would understand the changes she wanted to make to the family establishment. For thirty years, the restaurant had been owned and operated in pretty much the same way. She just wanted to bring the diner into modern times.

As she walked through the small kitchen toward her office, she made a mental note of the machinery that needed upgrades. None of the gauges on the equipment worked properly. Discernment was as much a part of the cooking process as the recipes.

Heating temperatures had either to be approximated or guessed. But as luck would have it, most of the cooks and wait staff had been loyal to the Williams family. They knew how to work everything as well as or even better than Kayla did.

But this was no way to run a business. With a sigh, she began to turn on the grills and the oven. *One oven,* she thought. How had her mom done it? The restaurant served breakfast, lunch and dinner. Pies, macaroni and cheese dishes by the dozens, casseroles, all came from the poor overworked *La Cornue* Anke had brought with her from Holland. Kayla loved the French appliance, but she needed more than one, which meant renovating the undersized kitchen space that was woefully inadequate for the number of meals the restaurant served on a daily basis.

The alarm on her watch sounded. In about thirty minutes, the rest of her small staff would arrive. She set the coffee maker to brew and then walked back to her office to review the weekend's reports. The aroma of the strong Arabica beans wafted back to her makeshift space, which made her feel more welcome. This was home.

Imagination was a wonderful thing, especially when used to dream. Kayla smiled. *One day,* she thought. Instead of the dark, closet-like room with the hand-me-down table that served as her desk, her mind's eye saw

5

Dangerous Dilemmas

a glass-topped bow desk with plenty of storage for files and reports and a plush leather chair behind it.

A gentle sigh escaped her lips. It could happen. She could achieve all of her goals if she saved, planned and didn't allow distractions to interfere with her life's ambitions. Kayla closed her eyes. *Okay, kid, get to work.* Mini pep-talk over, she settled down to do what she needed. In a few minutes, she was lost in her paperwork and the mundane details of running a business. A successful one despite its challenges, she had to admit.

What seemed like seconds later, she heard Tracey come in followed by the rest of the crew. Kayla had to admit that she had an excellent staff. Turnover was low, so there wasn't much to do by way of training. Everyone came in and performed their assigned tasks.

By 6:00 A.M., the Williams Family Diner was in full swing. A steady hum of activity, chatter, clanging and banging indicated everything was as it should be. Kayla continued working on the schedules, humming along to whatever song happened to be on the radio.

The aroma of sausage, bacon, cheese grits, hash browns, fried eggs and warm butter biscuits permeated the air. Yep, the construction crew was in. About ten guys with appetites big enough to put a whole squad of football players to shame filled the seats along the front counter. Every now and then she would hear snippets of their conversation. A shameless lot, this bunch of guys. Monday mornings were usually filled with the sexploits of the weekend.

"Yeah man, I got with Tina this weekend—gave it to her real good too."

Kayla blushed in her office.

"Uh huh, the only way you got a nut this weekend was with your hand, Carlo."

6

"Naw, baby, I got it with your sister. She took in all ten inches of this Colombian pipe, man. Yo, then she begged for more. But I told her no 'cause I had a date with your mama." A generous round of laughter followed that comment.

Tsk...tsk...boys will be boys. Kayla shook her head and went back to the keyboard of her 486 computer, the dinosaur her father had been so proud of when he purchased it.

He'd said, "Baby girl, with this new computer, we're going to step into the modern age of doing business. We can keep all our records right here. The computer will even replace the need for all these file drawers." He'd beamed as he said, "This will give us the edge over some of these other mom and pop operations. Mark my words." The memory of that conversation played around the edges of her consciousness.

Her father had fancied himself some sort of visionary back then. Of course, he never did learn how to use it properly, which meant she did most, if not all, of the accounting, bookkeeping and data storing.

During the occasional times when James did turn it on, he ended up in a battle with the darned machine. Battles the machine won and her daddy cursed it to hell.

"Oh, Daddy, how I miss you," she whispered.

Shush, baby girl, you're doing fine, she felt him say. A momentary calm allowed her to return to business, which gave a temporary reprieve to the wave of apprehension that washed over her.

She would have to make a decision. The right decision. But more importantly, she would have to learn how to stop second-guessing herself. Her parents had trusted her...that had to be good for something.

She had just selected the print button when a loud crash and a string of curses disturbed the peace of the morning. Kayla jumped from behind her work area to see what was going on in the kitchen. Flour and dough littered the small work area in front of the fryers.

"I'm sorry, Miss Kayla. The oil was hotter than I expected. I was rushing so fast to take the others out that I dropped the dough I was carrying after the first batch started to burn. I'm afraid I've ruined this whole batch of apple fritters. This will put us about twenty minutes behind schedule while I make more."

Par for the course. "Miss Maybelle, it's okay. I'll help you make the dough. Don't worry about it. We'll get it done."

Despite her other duties, Kayla washed her hands then put on an apron. She was chin deep in flour in no time.

The rest of the morning proceeded without too much of a hitch, and the next wave of regulars dined with no mishaps. Kayla was once again engrossed in her paperwork, where she took the occasional break to review her plans for the remodeling.

"You've folded and refolded those plans so many times I think the paper will fall apart," Tracey said as she caught Kayla during one of her mini breaks.

"I know, but I can't help it. Sometimes I just need something to hold on to...a little piece of the dream. What's going on out there?"

Tracey smiled. "Everything's fine. We're doing our part to feed the hungry citizens of Hilton Head. But I was wondering if you were okay. It's already 1:00 P.M.; 'Mr. Special' is almost finished with lunch. I think he's been looking for you—"

Before Tracey could finish, Kayla had jumped into high gear. She flicked her wrist upward to check the time on her watch. "Oh my gosh! I can't believe time got away from me like that. How do I look?"

Smirking, she said, "Like you run a restaurant. Now go before he has to get back to work. And this time ask him some questions. We need more information."

Kayla smoothed her hair, tucking it behind her ears. She ignored Tracey's last comment, but it lingered on her mind as she approached the seating area. *There he is...Damn this feels like eighth grade.*

Careful not to make eye contact with Cole too early, Kayla walked around to greet each customer one by one. Some she knew by name and asked about parents or kids. Families who had been patrons from the day the place opened still came into the diner. Some of the nervousness she felt melted away as she got into the groove. She sighed inwardly. Despite it all, this is what it was all about. Her customers.

"Miss Williams?"

Kayla was so surprised, she almost tripped into his arms. *Did he just call my name?* She stammered through her reply, hoping she didn't sound like too much of an idiot. "Hi there, is everything all right? How was your food?"

"Perfect as usual. I've been coming here for almost six months, and I haven't been disappointed yet. I just wanted to tell you what a fantastic job I think you're doing. I love the food and the atmosphere. It's hard to find a place that will give you such a personal touch." Cole extended his hand. "My name is Cole Lewis."

Grateful, Kayla accepted his hand and treated him to a generous smile. "Nice to meet you, Mr. Lewis. Thanks for giving us a try. I'm Kayla Williams, owner, chief, cook and bottle washer. I've noticed you're a pretty regular customer. Believe me, we love patron loyalty—so how about a piece of pie on me?"

Cole held up his hands. "I'm stuffed. Maybe another time, if you'll have a cup of coffee with me."

Charming. "So, what do you do?" Kayla asked innocently.

"Hmmm, answering a question with a question. I see I'm going to have to keep on my toes with you."

His even white smile made her heart skip a beat. She felt the moisture begin to pool between her legs, but as if that weren't bad enough, she had to carry on a conversation while her clit contracted wildly, almost demanding she jump the man right now. Kayla squeezed her thighs together as she forced her brain to concentrate on small talk.

With a devilish expression adding fire to his amber eyes, he said, "Answer my question and I'll answer yours."

Squeeze tighter. "I...uh...well...okay, sure. One cup of coffee." Kayla motioned for Gladys to bring coffee to the table and then sat down. All the excuses she regularly used to reject her male customers' advances flew out of her head. Instead, Kayla leaned back into the red fifties-style cushioned chair to enjoy the company of this very handsome young man.

"I promise I won't bite. Not on the first date anyway."

Good thing this is just coffee. Kayla smiled. "I'm sitting, which means I'm holding up my end of the bargain."

"And so you are." He took time to finish his Yankee pot roast, gently sliding the last spoonful of mashed potatoes on top before he opened his mouth to consume it. He seemed to make love to the fork before he released it from thick, well-formed, kissable lips.

Kayla struggled for self-control. His mouth was sexy enough, but dimples deep enough to swim in just about did her in. *Damn, why hadn't I noticed that before?*

Pushing his plate to the side, he cleaned his palate with a generous sip of water. "I am an editor and a writer. I don't want to sound like a commercial, but have you ever heard of *Full Flava Magazine*? It's a hip-hop culture magazine. We've been in print for five years and we're in the process of gearing up for the anniversary edition now. Anyway, I'm the cofounder and a co-owner."

"Oh my goodness, no wonder you look so familiar." Kayla snapped her fingers. "That's what it is. The picture in the magazine doesn't do you justice." The radiant smile she gave him lit up her face. *No wonder I can't get you off my mind.*

"Okay, so I take it you're a reader." The twinkle in his eyes sparkled brighter. It was nice to be recognized.

"I'm more than just a reader, I'm a big fan. Your magazine is my escape when I need something quick to read before I settle down into bed. Most of my time is taken up here, but I'm a regular subscriber…have been for a couple of years too. I get a real kick out of your weekly editorial column and your advice columnists. Tell me, those aren't real questions people send in, are they?"

His leaning forward was subtle, not a calculated move, but an effective one. Kayla felt her heart pumping to a samba beat the nearer he came. What was he trying to do to her? She stirred the coffee Gladys had just refilled for her, grateful for the distraction.

Cole chuckled. "Of course they are! Hey, I hold my magazine to the utmost integrity. However, I will admit there are times when I slightly massage the nature of the question to fit the theme of the issue, but the for the most part, our readers are very into the magazine. We receive tons of mail on everything...especially for our relationship gurus. Seems folks have a lot of questions about *sex*."

I'm sure they do, Mr. Lewis. I'm sure they do.

"Listen, I have to get back to my meeting, but I'd love to continue this over...dinner...tomorrow?" The disarming smile he favored her with increased the contractions in her lower region.

Witty repartee was impossible as she groaned out her response. "I'd love to. Just give me a call here at the restaurant later on to discuss the details. Do you need the number?"

"Nope, I'm good." Cole placed the money for his meal on the table then stood up. "Fantastic, I'll see you at 8:00 P.M."

Squeeze tighter. Kayla sat back in her chair. *Good lawd, what have I just done?*

Tracey barely waited until Kayla made it back to her office before she pounced. "Okay, give me all the dirt."

An errant hair had to be tucked behind her ear before she addressed her friend's question. "I'm not sure I know what you're talking about."

"Oh hell no! You don't get to be coy with me. I know you haven't been laid in at least six months, probably longer, so don't act like sitting next to that fine-assed man is a daily occurrence. I want the play-by-play."

Giggles were heard all the way into the kitchen. Kayla acquiesced before they created any more of a scene. "Okay, okay, but keep your voice down. The gist of it is we had a nice chat during the remaining fifteen minutes of his lunch and then he invited me to dinner."

"Yes, yes, yes!" Tracey squealed. "Wear something red because it brings out the green in your eyes. And make sure you leave your hair down so it just graces your shoulders, and for goodness sakes, add a little color to those lips—no clear lip gloss tonight." She tapped her pointer finger to her mouth. "Now, what to wear? I think it should be short to show off those mile-long legs you sport under those drab clothes. But, we don't want it to be too sexy. Not on the first date anyway. So, where is he taking you?"

With a shrug, Kayla answered honestly, "I have absolutely no idea."

CHAPTER TWO

What was it about production meetings that dragged an hour's worth of discussion into an all-day affair? Not that it would have made much of a difference after today's lunch. Cole's attention was focused squarely back at a little diner on Highway 46. Kayla's southern lilt washed over him like a smooth ocean breeze…full of warmth and genuineness.

He could imagine her cooing in his ear like a southern belle as he drove deep inside of her curvaceous hips. Cole wanted her to say very naughty things to him, tell him what a good lover he was and how he satisfied her every desire. She would wrap her legs around his waist drawing him close…searing hot flesh against flesh. They wouldn't end until they were sweat soaked and sated. *Whew! Where the devil did that come from?*

"Mr. Lewis. Mr. Lewis? Are you all right, sir?"

Cole closed his eyes. The tightness between his legs had become altogether uncomfortable. "Yes, Martha. I'm fine, ah just a little distracted. How about we break for fifteen minutes? I need to make some calls." He closed his portfolio, but he needed a couple minutes before he could stand up. The muscles in his jaw flexed as he gritted his teeth. *You're a grown man, for heaven's sake.*

"I know that look," Robert teased. He knew that good taste dictated he leave it alone, but he did not intend to let his best friend off the hook. "What's her name? And promise me that it's not Sheila distracting you that way."

Man, if you only knew. "Funny." Cole leaned back in the chair to make himself more comfortable. "What makes you think I'm distracted by a woman? Have I mentioned anyone lately?"

Unimpressed, Robert responded, "Like that would make a difference. You get that same faraway look in your eyes every time. Furthermore, I've been watching you have the same reaction since you first laid eyes on the shapely and voluptuous Mrs. Shultz in fifth grade. She had you *taking the zero* twenty years ago, and by the looks of things, someone else has you doing it again."

His rude chuckle forced Cole to look down. Robert howled even louder once he realized he had been able to fool his friend so easily. "Bro, you got it bad. So, while your indifference may work on everybody else, it don't do a thing for me man 'cause I know ya."

Cole smirked. "Didn't I call for a break? Why are you still in here bothering me? I'm sure Cassandra could use your help with *something*." Ready to make it back to his office, he rose from the seat. Robert's comments had hit too close for comfort. He needed to clear his head.

But Robert refused to take the hint and followed him stride for long stride to the executive office at the end of the hall.

There was something to be said for not working with your best friend. Cole shook his head. Robert was nothing if not tenacious. Now that he'd picked up a scent of something, he wouldn't let it go, but frankly, Cole wasn't up to the battle right now.

Cole sat down then looked pointedly at his friend. "This is not the time and I'm definitely not in the right frame of mind for this discussion. Besides, we have a lot to do." Cole lowered his voice. "However, if you must know, I'm interested in someone, but I haven't made a play for her yet." Cole paused. "I'm not sure I want to deal with a relationship with everything that's going on in my life. If we're putting out an expanded edition in just a few short months as we've planned, we *both* need to focus on the work."

Robert held up his hands. "Don't look at me that way—my stuff is golden. The sales department has been selling ads like nightsticks to cops. And the checks are signed and in the mail. I can't help it if I know how to keep my woman satisfied and keep my business straight." Robert continued while he pumped his groin in his best John Witherspoon impression.

14

Cole half expected him to say, "Bam, bam, bam. Don't hate the playa, just 'cause you can't do the same." Cole smirked while his partner carried on. Fortunately for the magazine, Robert had a gift for gab that brought in more than adequate ad revenue to cover the extra pages planned for the anniversary issue.

"You wanna have a beer while we catch the Monday night game? You probably just need some down time to help you get motivated. A little de-stress to help clear out the cobwebs. Not that we're doing too badly. The anniversary issue is going to be off the chain just based on what we have going on already. I'm looking forward to the party too…especially the after-party with the bevy of beauties who will be in attendance."

"I'm sure you are. But about tonight, I can't, got too much to do. I'll take a rain check for the weekend. Maybe we can catch a USC Gamecocks game."

"That's fine. Saturday it is. Cassandra and I have plans for Sunday. But if you get bored or just need to talk, holla at your boy."

A grateful smile crossed Cole's lips. Despite his outlandish behavior at times, Robert was and had always been a good friend. They'd been through it all: the breakups, the make-ups, being broke and now riding high on the success of their dreams.

Moreover, Robert was right about the magazine. All that remained for the success of this project was for Cole to live up to his end of the bargain, which meant the content. His primary responsibility for the celebration was to handle the special features, to include some of his own *Editor's Choice* interviews.

After his earlier conversation with Kayla at the diner, he had half a mind to do something out of the ordinary with the advice columns. Maybe do a special call for reader questions…or maybe even a live chat. The idea percolated in his head as he lost himself in thought. *What you do to me Kayla.*

Cole raked his fingers through his hair. The job would be made much simpler if he could concentrate. It seemed every time the damned wind blew, his thoughts turned toward sex. Unfortunately, the lovely Ms.

Williams wouldn't change that one iota. Not the way he had been thinking about her. Thoughts of sex were probably going to increase and she would be the main attraction in his dreams.

Already, Cole found it difficult to edit at night when the first words that came to mind were *hot* and *horny*. Sometimes the text blurred and all he could see was the face of Ms. Williams. *Kayla*. He liked the way her name rolled off his tongue.

Even with flour in her hair, she was the most luscious young woman he'd run across in a long while. He chuckled quietly. There was something sexy about a woman who didn't mind getting her hands dirty. A nice change from the diva behavior and attitude of his ex-girl, Sheila Pickwell, Cole thought.

"Damn man. You've got it bad." Robert watched his friend in amusement. "If you don't find a way to hit it, you ain't never going to get anything done." He looked down at his watch. "Speaking of which, we'd better get back to the conference room. Janessa is up next. Sista knows her job, but if she tries to go through another three-hour cover presentation, I'm going to fire her ass."

They walked back to the conference room together. As soon as he sat down, Cole thought, *round two*.

Mercifully, the meeting only lasted another four hours. They had the cover design in place, the ads, submissions for several feature articles and the new layout for the issue. Cole couldn't have been more pleased with his team.

There was a cloudless evening sky as Cole drove home to his condominium. Even though he'd lived there for three years, the beauty of the development never failed to impress. A transplant from New York, he hadn't thought he would be able to adjust to the slower pace of Hilton Head, South Carolina, but this was definitely home. What had once just been thought of as a tourist town had now become a safe haven, so to speak. The water views, slower pace and friendly neighbors were a welcome change after a long day at work dealing with writers, entertainer's egos and frantic deadlines.

As time went on, Cole realized he missed the hustle and bustle of New York less and less. The place was still pure energy with an indefinable magic, but he was content just to visit his birthplace now. There was no need to live in New York, not when he had all this. Hilton Head had become a place where he could put down his roots. *Roots? Where the hell did that come from?*

Cole shook his head clear of such thoughts as he drove down Wide Water Road into his gated subdivision. The neighborhood contained an interesting mix of residents, from the up and coming professional to the retiree. That's probably what prompted such uncharacteristic thoughts, he told himself as he pulled his BMW X5 into the garage.

As soon as he reached the garage door, he began to slip off his shoes to leave them at the door. The first contact between his black-socked feet and the wood floors of his condominium began to push away the tension. He headed directly for his home office and put his laptop and portfolio case down on the desk before walking straight to the kitchen.

Dinner was going to have to be quick to allow him time to catch up with work. Come what may, tonight was a writing night. If he didn't get it together, he would be uncomfortably behind in his schedule.

Unfortunately, he had been so busy at work that the pickings were slim in both the refrigerator and freezer. Cole exhaled. He had a couple of choices if he intended to eat tonight—they were to order in or go pick it up. Or…go back to the Williams Diner…Now that was a pleasant idea.

"You cannot be this whooped, bro," he chastised himself. It was one thing to be interested, but another to be handicapped and consumed by thoughts. Cole reached into the nearly empty fridge for a cold Smirnoff Triple Black. The crisp, clean, refreshing taste of the drink beckoned to his lips, which he gladly obliged by taking a long sip.

He thought about how he would drink in Kayla's nectar after kissing her lower lips to fullness, then lick up her juices as she flowed freely for him. Her gentle moans of passion would turn to feral, guttural groans as he brought her to orgasm. *Umm...yeah...a nice long sip.*

This wasn't going to work for him. Not even Sheila had this kind of effect on him. What was it about Kayla that drew him in and refused to let go? Determined, Cole picked up the phone to order a pizza. He would stay in to do what he needed. Delicious, delightful and enchanting Kayla Williams would have to release her hold on him long enough for him to finish his business.

Bottle in hand, Cole headed toward his bedroom on the second level of his condo. The large master bedroom was the ultimate in bachelor hood-dom. The decorator he'd hired had taken his love for strong colors and used them throughout the space.

His king-sized bed was made out of hardwoods with a leather inset headboard and footboard. It effortlessly held his six foot two inch build with plenty of room for company. The bed was easily his favorite part of the room. But the pièce de résistance was the bay windowed sitting area, which afforded him a picture perfect view of the water in the back of development. Many a night the soothing sounds of the water calmed the tensions of the day.

After a quick shower, he changed into a muscle shirt and lightweight cotton shorts. Once he moisturized his lean, solid body, he felt human again. Now he was ready...

Water usually did the trick for him, which was part of the reason he'd paid extra to have a lake view. He went back downstairs, feeling much more refreshed and able to concentrate. Cole finished the drink, tossed the bottle in the kitchen trash, and then made his way back toward his office to get started. Noting that he still had some time to wait for his food to arrive, Cole lit the two large sandalwood candles that sat on either side of his executive style desk, turned on the CD player, and settled in to edit the first article.

The soothing sounds of the smooth jazz mix he'd made settled his nerves. Back in the zone now, he'd finished two short pieces before the grumble from his stomach reminded him of his order. Fifteen minutes later, he heard a welcome knock on the door.

"Hi lover," Sheila drawled before she dropped the raincoat and walked naked into his living room. Her long, light brown weave flowed gracefully to the middle of her exposed back.

Oh hell no! Cole closed his eyes. *What part of "it's over" didn't she understand?* Cole bent to pick up the coat then prayed for patience as he followed her into *his* living room.

"I believe you left this?" His tone dripped sarcasm. "Please put it back on. You're leaving now."

She leaned back on his black leather couch then uncrossed her legs to allow him a generous view of her *assets*. Her newly clean-shaven assets, he couldn't help but notice. His imagination immediately worked overtime. Sheila's long brown tousled weave and flawless pecan-brown skin against the backdrop of the sleek, black couch created quite an exotic African safari picture. Inwardly, Cole groaned. She was having just the effect on him she wanted. But he was determined that common sense would prevail over carnal desire. And he damned sure wasn't going to let her see him sweat.

Cole cleared his throat. *Lord, did I do something I shouldn't have?* "Sheila, I'm doing my best to be patient with you, but if you need me to, I can spell it out for you. I want you to stop coming to my house uninvited, and I want you to stop playing these childish games. Show a little more maturity, please." *And a lot less skin.*

With a twist of the hair she wound around her fingers, she said, "You never used to mind when I showed up wearing my little coats before. Why are you being so cold, Cole? And since when have you ever turned *this* down?" Sheila sucked on two fingers, then used them to tease a pointed soft brown nipple to a taut peak. Her breasts jutted out, begging for his attention.

Just get to the damn door. Cole gulped. His struggle for self-control neared capacity. "Five seconds, Sheila. If you're not out of here, I'll have your naked ass arrested for trespassing."

As if calling his bluff, she placed two fingers in her mouth again, this time allowing them to languidly create a path from her full breasts to her shaven apex. Sheila tasted herself then teased her bud to life. Several strokes later, her sharp intake of breath indicated she was close to orgasm. From her mouth to her quivering lips, then from her lips to her mouth, she moved her fingers back and forth until she found release.

Seemingly permanently rooted to the same spot in front of the doorway, Cole watched but didn't make a move toward her. At this point, he couldn't if he wanted to. Human nature made it impossible for him not to react to the sight of his beautiful ex-girlfriend. He was so hard he could barely breathe.

His hand dropped casually down to his pulsating bulge. But he caught himself mid stroke through the thin fabric of his athletic shorts. The little voice that kept him out of trouble was practically shouting at him...telling him to be strong. Most of all, it told him to keep his mind focused on the lessons he'd learned in the past. The reason for the break up of the relationship came screaming back into focus. Namely, her barracuda-like personality.

Sheila had a great appetite for men she felt could help her advance. Never one to do anything as *pedestrian* as work, she depended on beauty to achieve her goals. According to her track record, she was one to use men only for as long as they were useful, and then they were chewed up and spat out. Cole, on the other hand, had been the victim of her constant betrayal. There was some question as to whether fidelity was even in her vocabulary—which was drama he did not need or want.

Despite the temptation she presented, Cole decided, rather than complicate his life by tangling with her again, he'd rather chew nails. Anything was better than going back to what he'd previously had with her. The sex was good, but not at the cost of his soul.

Finally, Sheila stood up, but she didn't put on the raincoat. Instead, she sashayed to the door wearing nothing but a "gotcha" cat grin. As she passed she licked her plum colored lips slowly. "Good night, lover. Think about me."

The pizza delivery arrived at the door at the same time, giving the male driver a much bigger tip than he'd ever imagined.

"What are you looking at?" she said as she looked the poor young man up and down. A trail of Red Door perfume followed her out.

Instinctively, Cole inhaled long and deeply. The sexy fragrance was one of his favorites, which Sheila knew damned well.

The young deliveryman looked from Cole to Sheila, and then back to Cole, who just shrugged.

"Don't ask," he said as he paid for the food.

Sheila took one last look backward and then squealed the tires of her new Aquarius Blue Volkswagen Beetle out of Cole's driveway. She may have lost this battle, but she definitely hadn't lost the war, judging from his *reaction* to seeing her again. He'd stared so hard, she could almost feel his touch. *Don't worry, lova, I'll be back.*

Despite the temperature, she made the short drive to her home in the buff. If anyone saw her driving down Wide Water Road, they'd just be in damn luck like the pizza boy, she thought. Right now, she just wanted to enjoy the feeling of the air against her heated body, along with the sense of freedom she felt as her long weave blew in the cool evening breeze.

Cole had never treated her like this before. Even mad, he would always give in to the way she liked to make up after a fight. No doubt, once he remembered their nights of passionate lovemaking right on the same couch she'd just left, he would call her.

The car was a gift from a very nice, very wealthy old man, unfortunately one even Viagra couldn't help. Damn, why had Cole turned her down when she needed him? Needed the way he loved her until she was hoarse from screaming out his name in guttural passion. Yeah, she needed him bad. With one hand on the steering wheel, with one hand on the steering wheel, she sucked the fingers on the other one.

Decision made. She would just have to continue to work on his resolve until he saw it her way. *This isn't over by a long shot, lover boy.*

Dangerous Dilemmas

The pizza had arrived, but he'd lost his appetite—for food anyway. Nonetheless, he went to the kitchen to eat and to try to salvage the rest of the evening.

He grabbed another Smirnoff. Then, after he turned on his audio equipment in the living room, he changed the music from smooth and soothing jazz to very loud and boisterous rap. Considering certain parts of his anatomy were still *standing at attention*, it would be awhile before he could settle back down to work.

In case he wondered whether it were bad enough before Sheila came over, he had confirmation now that he needed some good lovin' and soon! He suppressed the urge to daydream about Kayla as he ate the now room temperature pepperoni pizza. After two slices, he put the rest of the pie in the refrigerator and went back to his office. If he were lucky, he might be able to get in a couple hours of real work before settling in for the evening.

He opened the first letter to the editor. Cassandra had arranged them according to interest. *Dear Editor,*

I love your magazine, but I'd like to see more focus on current issues.

The magazine intended to begin a column with one of the professors from the college in Columbia to focus on politics and other areas of local interest.

He answered that letter and several others. And judging from the number of requests, romance seemed to be the most queried about topic. Cole skimmed through the large stack. Some questions were suited for use in the magazine, others…well others Cassandra must have put in the stack just to elicit a reaction from him. And he would deal with her in the morning.

Dear Editor,

I like Full Flava *magazine, but you need to spice it up more. I'd love to read more advice columns for those of us struggling with relationship issues.*

Your interviews with celebrities seem to be right on point and show us another side of the glitz, but it would be nice to read more about real life issues.

22

As a young college student, I'm always interested in the tips that work for other people. I'd also like to read about some new tips to spice up the bedroom.

Spicing up the bedroom...now, that's a nice thought. Long legs, perfect lips, a flat stomach, cat shaped green eyes, beautiful light brown complexion, high cheekbones and, last but certainly not least, an ass and breasts that totally capture his attention...firm, tight and just the right size.

What kind of lover would she be? Patient and gentle like her personality at the restaurant, as she milled around with the customers and talked with staff? Or was she more a tigress whose eyes would turn dark and sultry from desire while she pounced hungrily on her lover? Would Kayla want him to pump her hard and fast or slow and even? He felt himself lengthen.

And why are you having these thoughts when you haven't even had your first date?

Harder and longer still as his vision became more vivid, his erection strengthened like a hurricane gathering force in open water. Cole rubbed himself to soothe the ache that seemed determined to be satisfied only one way. "Down boy!" he scolded.

Forcing his attention back to his editorial duties, Cole worked until his eyes burned. The solid mahogany mantle clock indicated that it was 1:00 A.M. He figured he'd just have to burn the midnight oil again after his dinner date with Kayla.

Cole looked down at the stack of articles and letters he'd completed as compared to the ones he still needed to go through. Between his erotic thoughts of Kayla and Sheila's buck-naked shenanigans, he'd barely scratched the surface of what he'd planned to get done.

Muddling through, he read one last letter to the editor. This email started out similarly to the last one about spicing up future issues. The reader wanted the magazine to do a feature on African American lingerie specialty stores. *Kayla in a deep burgundy, lace demi bra and thong.* Maybe...

Sex sells, so if he could find a lingerie store to fit the bill located close to Hilton Head, he would entertain the thought of a feature. Readers determined the success of the magazine, and he definitely wanted to make them happy.

Cole released a long harsh breath, then logged off the computer and blew out the candles. The music went next...followed by his resolve not to think about sex again tonight.

Before he could change his mind, his hand sought the growing bulge between his legs. By the time Cole reached his bed, he was breathing heavily from the need to satisfy his own desire.

He leaned back against the strong headboard. Dropping his shorts to the side of the bed after he removed them, he grasped his thick, stiff member in his hand. His strokes were long and impatient; the fire had burned slowly the majority of the day. Cole worked his hand up and down, down and up until he felt the first tremors...mild at first, then he squeezed tighter, increasing the pressure all the way to his tip until he couldn't last another second.

Ughh...he panted breathlessly along with his climax.

CHAPTER THREE

It was almost midnight by the time Kayla felt like crawling into bed from pure exhaustion. After serving the last customer, there was still the clean up and the beginning of the week inventory to do before she locked up for the night. It was something she preferred to do in solitary. The staff had more labor to do during the day than she did, so inventory was a burden she resigned herself to completing. She left the restaurant at 11:00 P.M., just enough time to get some rest before starting all over again.

Eighty-hour work weeks were par for the course...for now anyway, she thought with a long sigh, as she reached the large oak front door to her bungalow-style home. Something had to give. The pace was unhealthy and self-defeating.

Once inside, Kayla moved through her house with more of a sense of purpose, intent as she was to dip her body under the relaxing cascade of shower water as soon as possible. She selected a Miles Jaye CD and listened to him croon in the background as she lit several citrus and melon candles between her bedroom and bathroom.

The private space she created in her home was designed to soothe and relax. Her boudoir, as she referred to it, was indeed her sanctuary. When nothing else went right—something broke at the restaurant, her car needed repair, or some other minor emergency happened—she always had a soothing place to retreat.

"I've been a fool for you..." played in the background as she moved from the bedroom to the bath. In the shower, Kayla let the hot water meander down her back. The heady scent of her floral body wash combined with her sensual thoughts caused her to feel more than a hint of disappointment that she was in the shower alone instead of with sexy Cole Lewis from the restaurant.

Dangerous Dilemmas

Since Cole had begun to come into the restaurant about six months ago, he hadn't strayed too far from her thoughts—especially her more erotic musings, which had dramatically increased of late. She wanted to feel Cole next to her, his body melded against hers as she aligned her soft curves with the muscled strength of his masculine physique.

Kayla sighed again and turned the dual showerheads to full blast. The heat oozed the pain away from her tired muscles. She turned her back to the water to wet her long tresses. As she worked the shampoo into a luscious lather, she imagined Cole's fingers dancing in her hair. A tiny puff of air escaped her lips...

The vision continued while he lathered her hair, gently but insistently. He helped her rinse out the soap, slowly directing the bubbles over her erect nipples. She felt his hands gently squeeze the light brown buds until they were hard, stiff peaks. He blazed a trail over her pulsating body, which ignited her entire being and awakened in her a wantonness she hadn't ever experienced. *Ummm...if you're half as good as in my dreams, I'm in serious trouble.*

"Dammit!" she huffed and abruptly turned off the water. "This is not going to happen, so just get over it." Their date would be a nice little excursion to break the monotony of life. That's all she would accept, but what it would not be is an excuse to do things...Her mind tried to conjure up the right word.

Irresponsible. Yes, that was it. She wouldn't allow raging hormones to break her resolve. The restaurant was enough to handle, and relationships complicated things. David had only been out of her life for a year. She hadn't turned into some desperate, horny old maid in that time. Okay...*horny* she would admit to.

September produced cooler nights now in Hilton Head. After her shower, Kayla dressed in a nightshirt and pants, then turned down the comforter and slipped between the cool sheets. *Heaven.* The bed felt divine, and the shower had relaxed her tired muscles, but now...Her restless mind continued to replay trials of her day.

"I have to ask you, was there a plan? I mean, did y'all ever think about what would happen to me?" she asked, looking toward the ceiling for answers. "There was only enough insurance coverage to pay for the funerals. So what am I supposed to do now?"

Maybe it was fatigue, maybe it was a part of the grieving process, but she was angry. Kayla wiped away a single tear of frustration. She hated the constant emotional battle she engaged in while she made decisions about the business—the war within to be the perfect daughter, to honor them without fail. As a result, she felt guilty for betraying her parents' memory.

Guilt...also because she faulted them for having each other to depend on while she had no one. She remembered plenty of conversations around the table to discuss plans for the future. Anke and James had a close enough relationship to share everything. She'd always admired that quality about their marriage. It worked for them and helped to keep the relationship going in the tough times. They could afford to continue to run the restaurant in an old-fashioned, backbreaking style as long as they were together and had the love and support of a loyal, loving staff. Clarabelle, her sister, Maybelle, Clarence and her two part-time employees, Gertrude and Percy, were still wonderful, but now they were older, and it was difficult to find workers willing to work long hours for what she could afford to pay.

The cold reality was Kayla knew she couldn't manage without making changes. It wasn't a matter of choice at this point. Changing was a matter of the restaurant's survival. She hoped her parents would understand, but Kayla could just imagine them turning over in their graves from all the changes she planned to make.

For the most part, she'd had a good relationship with her parents, but there were times when they butted heads. Unfortunately, before their passing, modernization had been a point of contention between them.

He mother still thought she was in old world Holland and preferred doing everything the old-fashioned way, which usually meant a lot slower and by hand—spaghetti dinners made from sauce cooked all day long and fresh handmade pasta. Anke's small marble slab where she kneaded the dough was still used by Clarabelle. In the last several years, nothing had been discarded or traded in for a newer model—not processes, people, or products.

Kayla fluffed the pillow. But the pace for a single proprietor was different from what they'd experienced in sharing the responsibilities. Not to mention, on top of the fact that her parents had had each other to lean on, they'd also had her.

"I've just got me and I'm scared." *There, I've said it.*

In response, she heard, *It's going to be all right.*

Wasn't what she had in mind to change the name, menu and method of cooking better than losing the business altogether, she reasoned with herself? Kayla watched the ceiling fan spin. The slow swirling motion seemed to keep time with her ever-changing thoughts.

Out of the blue, she wondered what her parents would think of Cole. *Now, you're really losing it.* Kayla chuckled. James would give Cole the third degree, but he would get a kick out of the fact that he too owned a successful business. And it wouldn't hurt that he was also a writer. Daddy had always wanted to pen a cookbook of some of his favorite recipes, but there was always so much work to do. Kayla sighed. Now there would never be any more time.

Time…why did we always take it for granted? Kayla looked at the clock on her nightstand beside her bed and almost cringed. She only had about three hours sleep coming to her before it would be time to start her hectic schedule all over again. Without more sleep, she suspected she might be a bumbling idiot during their date.

*Concentrate…relax…*Kayla closed her eyes. *Inhale…exhale… uhmmm…*Blocking out all other thoughts, she focused on the sound of Cole's velvety edged, bass voice—the strength and depth of which sent ripples of awareness coursing through her. *Why did he have to be so damned sexy?*

4:00 A.M.

Kayla covered her head with her satin-covered pillow and groaned.

"I'm not ready!" She lay in the bed for several additional minutes. Slowly, she reached up to touch the edges of her hair. *Damp.* The dream came back into focus. "Oh, gawd, you are pitiful!" How was she ever going to face him tonight after she had imagined such explicit escapades?

Like a scene from a bodice-ripper romance book, she told him exactly what she wanted. And she wanted him hard and rough. *Savagely, he took her from behind, holding her by the hips as he pumped into her. She could hear the sound of his body against hers. Slap, slap, slap. Her melon-sized breasts jiggled to the beat of their rhythm.*

He moved one hand from her hip to tease her sex as he drove deep, in and out of her tight lips. Kayla would work her hips against his body, pulling him more into her. Then she would turn the tables and ride him like the beautiful black stallion that he was. Finally, her screams of passion would mix with his grunts of desire until their perfect, mutual orgasm.

Squeezing her legs together to quell the throbbing of her sex, she lay still under the sheets. *Ten more minutes.* The ceiling fan over her bed sent cool air over her desire heated body. Before she could even think of moving, Kayla needed time to collect herself.

"Lord, let this day work out okay and don't let me make an ass of myself. Amen." The quick prayer was enough to get her moving. Kayla hopped out the bed, ready to face her day. And ready to face Cole.

6:00 A.M.

"Ooh whee, I haven't seen that look in a long while."

"I'm just so sure I have no idea what you're talking about."

Tracey put one hand on a narrow hip. "Um…hmm. I'd say someone had a good night. No offense, but you usually come in looking like something that the cat dragged in. Today…hmmm…I'd say you were almost glowing." Tracey giggled mischievously. "Are you ready for tonight? I think a date with Mr. Hunkalicious would inspire a rosy glow in me too, so I don't blame you a bit."

"Do you have any shame at all?"

"Not a damn bit when it comes to a fine man and a good lay. And neither should you. I want you to promise me you're going to have a good time. Let those electrified, steel reinforced walls down long enough to enjoy the company of a very nice man."

Kayla rolled her eyes. "Girl, you have problems!"

Tracey shrugged, her auburn hair gently gracing her shoulders as she did. "Call me crazy, but my nights are filled with Damon working the pipe like a master plumber."

Heat rose to Kayla's cheeks from Tracey's open discussion of private matters. Fantasizing was one thing, but it was quite another to share your desires publicly. A feat Tracey had never had a problem doing. Usually, Monday mornings were filled with a recount of the sexual exploits and tales of Damon and Tracey. If believed, the couple did it all, to include threesomes, foursomes, and *more*.

The direction Kayla's thoughts had taken made the tips of her ears burn. She was sure she could learn a thing or two about sexual experimentation from them, but she didn't think she could bring herself to *hang out* with her friend. Although, Tracey would no doubt be happy to give her illustrated notes.

Toward the end of the day, Kayla's cell phone rang. She recognized the number as one from the bank. A wave of apprehension swept over her and then seemed to coil around her heart. The same heart that threatened to beat right out of her chest. "Hello?" Did that shaky voice really belong to her?

"Ms. Williams, this is Tabitha Smith. I'm calling from the loan department about the application you put in to expand your restaurant.

Mr. Stone would like to meet with you some time this week to discuss the details."

It had to be physically impossible to be any more nervous, Kayla thought as perspiration dampened her grip on the phone in her hand. She had to remind herself to breathe. *It's okay, if they were going to deny you, they would have just sent a letter.* Once she found her voice, Kayla finally croaked out, "I can make myself available anytime, just give me a time."

As she listened, she had to force herself to concentrate on the words coming out of Ms. Smith's mouth. A million thoughts raced through her mind. *Was this really it?* Could she finally begin to update her restaurant to make it the modern southern-style for which she'd longed? After scheduling the appointment for the following day at 2 P.M., she leaned back in her chair to absorb the moment.

"Ow, ow,ow. Ms. Kayla."

Moment over…guess it's back to work. "I'm coming, just give me a second." *Next crisis.* Kayla pushed away the notes on her desk and rose from her seat to head back to the kitchen.

The rest of the day seemed to fly by after the incident, for which Kayla was grateful. No more grease fires, nothing else was burned, no one was hurt, *and* the customers seemed satisfied with their food and service. A good day by anyone's standards. Kayla resisted the urge to utter a sigh of relief…heaven forbid she tempt fate this close to being able to leave.

Cole called to say he would meet her in the restaurant parking lot at 8:00 P.M. but had not come in for his daily lunch special.

At 6:00 P.M., she left the remainder of the dinner hour in the capable hands of her assistant manager to go home to get ready.

A suggestive smile crossed Tracey's thin lips. "I know it's been awhile since you went out with a man, so do I need to give you some tips?"

"That's okay, I think I can handle it without the sage words of my freaky friend." "Don't worry, I won't embarrass *us*. Besides, it's just a nice friendly dinner. What could go so wrong?"

"Plenty if you don't play your cards right! And remember what I said earlier. Enjoy yourself and don't be such a prude. Have some fun tonight. You deserve a break—you've been working your ass off here at the restaurant for far too long. If anyone deserves some time to be a little freaky, it's you." Tracey paused. "You know, I kind of missed him this afternoon. I was all set to pump him for information, but he didn't come in...brotha kinda ruined my plans. But, I'll expect your full written report in the morning."

"Tracey!"

Waving her hand dismissively, she continued, "Don't 'Tracey' me. I demand you to have fun. You'll burn out at this rate. You know I love you like my biracial half-sister, but you need to listen to reason."

Much like a dog with a bone, Tracey wasn't going to let go now that she'd started. "Don't let guilt continue to make you run yourself into the ground. When you're in a grave next to your parents, who will run this place? My last name ain't Williams...you feel me?"

Drama queen. "Yeah, I feel you." *Would rather not be having this conversation right now, but I'm with ya.* Kayla smiled patiently. "Now, can I go? I'm going to be late if I don't get a move on."

Tracey took a step back. "Message received. I'll lay off for now. At least until I hear all the good dish on what happens, but do me one favor, darlin'. Look out for number one 'cause in the end, if you don't, who will? If you have a good time with *Mr. Special*, don't hesitate to let him know it. Spread those wings, girl."

Shaking her head, she responded, "It's just dinner, but I'm with ya."

Kayla drove the short distance home, feeling anxious and jittery, but also filled with pleasant excitement. After a quick shower, she dressed in a red form-fitting spaghetti-strapped dress, an impulsive purchase made some weeks prior. The dress had been hanging in the back of the closet, waiting on that some day when it would be appropriate.

After she passed on several more conservative outfits, she decided tonight, why not? Kayla chuckled, sure that, with her scandalous behind, Tracey would approve of her choice.

All right now. After seeing her reflection, she took a deep breath. The plunging neckline hinted of the delight between her full-breasts. Sexy, without being overdone was the look she'd hoped for. Luckily, her assessment in the mirror proved she'd succeeded. *Nice.* After a spray of Coco Mademoiselle, she was ready to go. She smoothed the dress over her flat abdomen. Since she still didn't know where they were going, she had to hope she was dressed appropriately. *Guess we'll see what you're made of Mr. Lewis.*

Her carefully crafted sense of bravado began to crack around 7:30 P.M. The closer she came to taking that final step to leave the house, the more everything in her screamed for her to back out, be a coward. Fear and anxiety tied her stomach in square knots to rival any the best scout could make.

*Inhale…exhale…*After all, didn't she have a full enough life without adding more?

Unfortunately, she didn't have a cell phone number to call to cancel the date. It's just dinner; isn't that what she'd told Tracey? *The date…What are you doing going out with Cole, or anyone else for that matter, when you have so much else to do?*

Enjoy yourself for once, kitten.

With a start, Kayla looked around her bedroom. No one was there, but she would have sworn she heard her father's deep, well-modulated voice giving encouragement. Her shoulders slumped in defeat as she moved her head back to look up to the ceiling.

"Okay, okay. I'm going."

After one last check of her appearance, she grabbed her car keys off the dresser and walked to the garage. Kayla inhaled deeply and exhaled slowly. She placed the key in the ignition. Her hand shook slightly. "What if something goes wrong at the restaurant; maybe Tracey will need me tonight."

Go! she heard.

Dangerous Dilemmas

"All right...I'm going, I'm going."

Finally, she started the ignition of her laser-red Saab convertible. *It's now or never.*

CHAPTER FOUR

When Kayla returned to the parking lot of the diner, Cole was already there. Once he spotted her, he walked over to the car to open the door.

As soon as she stepped out her Saab, he said, "You look absolutely beautiful," in that smooth, sexy voice of his that she was quickly coming to adore.

"Ditto. You look very nice yourself." The gray Armani suit, light blue shirt and silver-colored silk tie perfectly complemented his fair coloring. And did she detect Armani Code? *Damn, he is making it hard for a sista.* She smiled to herself as sinfully wicked thoughts paraded through her mind. He guided her to his X5 to open the passenger door for her.

Kayla knew Tracey was probably inside the restaurant about to wet herself, but she resisted the temptation to go in to say something to her. Her friend was right. It was just one night. *What's more,* she thought as she ran her tongue in a slow, seductive manner over the sienna red covering her lips, *he was too much man to let go by without at least honoring this one request.*

Concentrate girl. Once seated, she said, "I've been so caught up in the affairs of the restaurant I forgot to ask a few pertinent questions. One of which is, so where are we going tonight? And am I appropriately dressed?"

Before he started the engine, Cole stole an appreciative glance at her. "I'd say perfectly."

His incredibly disarming smile pushed a sigh through Kayla's lips.

"And to answer your first question, sorry for all the mystery. I had to make a couple of calls. We're going to one of my favorite places to relax, *The Blue Note.* On Tuesdays, they play smooth jazz and serve a gourmet buffet as well as delicious hors d'oeuvres. So I hope you're hungry. I've known the owner, Beau Turner, for years, but I had to confirm we could get in."

Starving, but not for food. "Oh, that sounds wonderful. I haven't been there in quite a while, and yes, I know what you mean about getting a table. I've waited with friends for over two hours before on the weekends, but I've heard it's the same all the time."

Most times, Kayla preferred rhythm and blues and rap to smooth jazz, but tonight she was grateful for his choice. She wanted to chill, let the worries of the past few months roll off her back. Tomorrow was soon enough to get back to business. Tamia, Monica, Mary J. Blige and Heather Headley would have to do without her for one night while she planned to slow dance with Gerald Albright and Jonathan Butler.

"Good, so you forgive me for being circumspect?" Cole guided the vehicle onto Highway 46, and in no time, they headed toward Hardeeville.

"Considering your motivation, there's nothing to forgive. However, if you have more surprises in store in order to make up, please go right ahead." A smile lit up her face.

"Oh, I have all sorts of wonderful ways to make up. Any and all of which I'm willing to show you...all night long if you think you can handle it."

And the next point goes to Cole Lewis. Kayla closed her eyes and willed her heart to stay in her chest. "Well, maybe I'll let you off the hook this one time since you're being so nice."

His slight chuckle reverberated in the small space between them. Kayla sat back into the comfort of his leather seats. She needed to gather herself again. His strong masculine sensuality threatened to overwhelm her senses, especially paired with the confidence he exuded. Her breath caught in her throat.

By the time they walked into the club arm-in-arm, her heart had started to beat at the normal pace. All vanity aside, she had to admit they looked like the cover of one of his magazines. Cole moved like a man who was used to getting what he wanted. The vixen in her enjoyed the envious stares from other women and the appreciative looks from the male patrons.

When they reached the attendant, Cole paid their cover charges then guided her toward a reserved table close to the stage. As soon as they sat down, a server appeared.

"We've been expecting you, Mr. Lewis; so nice to see you again. What can I get you, sir?" she asked.

Feeling strangely possessive, Kayla said, "I'll have whatever he's having."

Cole studied her as he leaned back in the chair. Fluff or substance? Definitely substance. "We'll both have an Errol Flynn."

Kayla's smile lit up her face. "Very nice, Mr. Lewis, Cognac and Grand Marnier, such a nice combination together. And here I almost thought you would order one of those sweet Kool-Aid flavored martinis that have become so popular. I'll admit I'm pleasantly surprised. Cognac is one of my favorite drinks."

"Something else we share."

The first thing being? She wanted to ask, but didn't want to be rude. *All in due time*, she reminded herself. Cole had an intense but slow and easygoing personality. Rich like the cognac he'd just ordered, he was also smooth, bold, intelligent and strong. All qualities that, despite her earlier nervousness, made her feel calm and relaxed. And all that made him extremely attractive.

"So," Kayla, teased, "Do you always have that effect on women? The kind that makes a woman want to pay special attention to you?"

The dimples sprang to life as he leaned in toward her. "I don't know. Do I have that effect on you?"

Play with fire and you'll get burned. "Do you want to?"

Cole took her by the hand. "Let's dance."

He held her close, gently caressing the exposed skin of her back. Kayla leaned into his embrace as if she had belonged in his arms all her life. They danced close, feeling the rhythm of the music, feeling the rhythm of the lyrics, feeling the rhythm of their hearts.

Several songs later, they were still on the small dance floor. The magnetic energy that flowed between them made air a precious commodity. Finally, Kayla broke the spell. "I think we'd uh…better sit down now."

Cole exhaled. "I think you're probably right."

Kayla sipped her drink casually to allow the rich, full-bodied smoothness of the cognac to glide easily down her throat. After the third sip, warmth suffused her body. All of a sudden, the world became a very, very nice place.

"Thank you for tonight. I've been feeling a little down lately, so this is a welcome treat."

"No need to thank me. You've done me the honor of spending time with me. I should be the one expressing gratitude." Cole circled the rim of his glass. "Tell me more about you, Kayla Williams."

"There's not so much. I'm just a hard-working girl from a lovely little island in South Carolina." Mesmerized, she watched while he continued to caress the glass. She felt her breath catch mid-inhale. *Get a hold of yourself girl*, she commanded in a weak attempt to fight the wanton attraction that made her lips quiver from the desire to be kissed.

In reckless abandon, Cole made no attempt to hide the fact he was watching her. "I want to know more about you aside from the obvious, which is that you're gorgeous, intelligent, ambitious and sexy as hell."

Kayla blushed. "Thank you for the compliment. But there's really not much to tell." *Except maybe, I'd love for you to take me right here on this small table.* "My father, James Williams, was in the Air Force when he met my mother, Anke, in Rotterdam in the early seventies. My mom was funny, very traditional in some ways and then in others, she was a rebel without a clue. But she was my champion when I needed her to be." Kayla looked down. After a brief pause she continued. It was always tough to tell people about them. "They died in a car accident three years ago."

"I'm sorry, Kayla." Cole lifted her head then held her gaze.

Quietly, she said, "It's okay. I still miss them like hell, but I'm making it. I've got the restaurant to keep me plenty busy. There's always something to do, and the hours I work are pretty demanding, which I'm sure you know all about with the magazine."

Shaking off the negativity of talking about her parents, she leaned toward him. "Tell me how you got started. I think what you do is fascinating, and all the people you must get to meet…that must be so exciting."

"I love what I do, but my real joy comes from doing what I'm doing right now. I love to talk to people, hear their stories. I've always been intrigued by the human spirit."

"Uh oh, should I be careful about what I say?" Kayla teased. "Am I being interviewed? Is all this on the record?"

"You are definitely not being interviewed, though I think you'd make an excellent human interest story. Tonight, you're all mine."

As if to punctuate his point, he stroked the side of her face with the pad of his thumb.

A shudder of hot desire passed through her from the simple touch.

"Is there anything I can do about you feeling down? I'm not being flippant; I want to help."

"You already are." A small smile gave him reassurance. "Sometimes I get in such a rut with so much to do at the restaurant, at times I don't know if I'm coming or going. I'm just on autopilot, doing what needs to be done. Tracey, my assistant manager, thinks it's because I don't go out enough. Needless to say, she was thrilled about tonight. I'd say, the next time you come in, expect some extra-special service."

"Count on it. Wednesday is stewed beef with new potatoes—you know I'll be there. Hell, I'd let the magazine burn down before I missed that."

"You are incorrigible!" Kayla shook her head and giggled. "When was your first trip to our little establishment?"

Cole sat back in his chair to think. "Six months ago on a Friday. I had the fried fish, hush puppies, slaw, macaroni and cheese. I called my mom from the restaurant to tell her I was never coming home again. I've tried to come in every day since then. The only time I miss is when I have a meeting that runs long or I'm out of town. I think I'm going to start the Williams Diner fan club next."

There was that devilish smile again. "Um…um…um…has anyone ever told you that you have no sense?" Kayla brought her hand to her mouth to stifle her laughter. Between the cognac and Cole, she was feeling no pain. Since he'd successfully helped her overcome the blues—she didn't know how the evening could get any better.

Kayla held up her hands in surrender. "Now, tell me all about the magazine for real this time. You're going to make me rip this tight dress with your silliness. I don't think it is designed for laughter."

"Hmmm, well as long as it was ripped in all the right places…" His infectious grin had her reacting the same way. Kayla felt as if she were talking with an old friend instead of someone she'd just met.

Before Cole began, he signaled for another drink. "When I created *Full Flava Magazine,* I knew I wanted to market to young, working-class African Americans. I wanted to cover contemporary issues from relation-ships to careers to politics to travel. I'm proud to say, I have a small but amazing staff, and we're adding new features all the time. Our fifth anniversary issue launches in about four months." His amber eyes were alive with interest as he spoke.

Kayla could sense his commitment, almost feel his passion. "I'm not just saying this because we're talking, but I really do like the magazine. I think you do a wonderful job, especially with your celebrity interviews and focus on local folks. You've done good for South Carolina."

"Thank you. We've been doing this for quite some time. In my humble opinion, it's going to be all that and then some." Cole continued. "We're hosting parties, town hall live chats, sort of like you see with Tom Joyner's Sky Shows. Anyway, you name it…we're doing it. All of Hilton Head is going to be talking about the national magazine that's sitting right in their backyard." Cole paused to sip his drink. "I'm not boring you am I? Sometimes, I get so wrapped up in this I forget not everyone shares my zeal. I've always loved the written word, music, painting and other mediums of art. I can get wrapped up I know, so when I do, just reel me back in."

Kayla grinned. "Don't be silly. I love hearing the enthusiasm in your voice when you talk about your work. We share a true passion for our careers. But don't let me distract you. Tell me more about your plans."

The second round of drinks arrived at the table. Kayla took a generous sip of hers while she listened.

Cole went on to give her more details, but then after talking for a bit longer, he changed the focus. "I can't let you off the hook so easily. You gotta tell me what makes Kayla Williams tick."

Kayla favored him with a capricious smile. "Dreams."

"Passionate nighttime dreams where a handsome young man who bears a striking resemblance to myself takes you in his arms—"

And rips my dress off. "Mr. Lewis, will you be serious?"

"Fine, but will you answer my question before we dance again?"

"Okay, okay, but don't laugh. I'm about to pour out my heart to you." She held the glass in both hands as if for support. After a long exhale, she continued. "For as long as I can remember, I've had what most folks would consider to be an overactive imagination. I see things in my mind's eye all the time. When I walk into a room or a building, house you name it, I see all the possibilities of that space." *Okay, try not to sound like too much of a kook.* "I have a dream book, which contains an architectural rendering of the restaurant and of all the new equipment I want, etc. I also have pictures of my dream house and furniture. There's just something about looking ahead instead of backward when it comes to the tangible things of life. I love to contemplate the future. I don't know…it gives me hope." Suddenly feeling as if she were talking too much, Kayla paused.

"That's very nice." Cole smiled. "I don't think it's funny at all. I like it, just one more thing to make you unique. I admire your dedication to the family business as well. But, don't stop, I want to hear more. How long have you been involved with the restaurant?"

Kayla sipped her drink before she continued. "All my life really. The diner has been in that same spot for thirty years. It had been a run down, old country store, but my parents gutted it and turned it into the diner you see today. I've always helped out. I think I've been cooking since I was two years old. But after I finished college, go Tigers, I came back to work full time in the restaurant."

"Clemson Tigers, huh? I'm a USC graduate myself. And don't even start, unless you want an all out war."

Kayla laughed. "Yeah, how about those USC chickens?"

"Hey, I warned you. They are not chickens; they're *cocks*." Cole casually stroked her hand while he spoke. "Cocks don't lay eggs. Nonetheless, we are very proud of our heritage. No matter what kind of fowl."

"Yeah, but is it foul or fowl?" Kayla tried hard not to concentrate on the feeling that threatened to overwhelm her from his touch. She trembled slightly.

"You are a delight, Kayla Williams. Tell me how many times you've been in love. I know someone so passionate has to have been at least one time in life."

After another sip of her drink, she answered honestly, "Just once, and it was a mistake." Kayla's eyes darkened. "His name is David Sutton, and I should never have allowed myself to fall for him."

Interest piqued, Cole released her hand as he sat back in the chair. "Do you think when we fall for someone, as you say, that we have a choice? Maybe I'm just a romantic, but I think love, attraction, even lust just happens, and we don't have any control over who our bodies or hearts pick."

Kayla chuckled. "I don't know if I would call that exactly a romantic notion, but I hear what you're saying. I guess I think on some level we should be able to stop ourselves from making a huge mistake with the person we are seeing. I mean, I guess I should have put the brakes on my relationship with David as soon as I realized it wasn't going to work out between us."

Cole shook his head. "Don't beat yourself up over it. I had a similar relationship with my ex-girlfriend, Sheila Pickwell. It was hot and heavy for a few months before I finally realized all she really wanted from me was access to my contacts in the music and film industry to further her dance career. I've been flying solo since then, almost a year."

Kayla shuddered. "Okay, no more talk about exes. I don't want to spoil this wonderful evening. Let's dance again."

Will Downing sang, "…a million ways to please a woman…"

As soon as Kayla was in Cole's arms again, she felt her body heat rise. Soon the only sound she could hear was the staccato beat of her heart, or was it Cole's? She didn't know any longer.

He absently stroked the sensitized skin along her spine while they danced close. Driven by desire, her body inched closer to his. If he didn't kiss her soon, she wouldn't be responsible for her actions.

Cole was approximately five inches taller than she…and from the feel of things, very blessed! Kayla felt his arousal near her abdomen.

Before he leaned in to capture her mouth, Cole looked into the smoldering depths of her eyes to seek permission. In response, Kayla leaned her mouth toward his waiting lips.

Cole planted a deep and passionate, soul-stirring kiss that was…almost possessive.

Kayla couldn't breathe. He was trying to take all of her, own her. Just the way she had envisioned he would in her fantasies about him.

When they finally came up for air, both gasped. Her knees shook, nearly buckling under his power. To steady herself, Kayla settled back into his secure embrace. *What is this man trying to do to me?*

He looked at her, his eyes asking permission to do it again. To answer, she simply reached up to him to initiate the kiss, enjoying her own eager response to him.

In a raspy voice, he asked, "Your place or mine?"

Game over, sexy Cole Lewis wins. "I'm close."

He handed her the keys. "Drive."

The waitress had left the check on the table while they were on the dance floor. Cole hurriedly took care of it, then turned his attention back to Kayla. They barely managed to make it out of the club. Cole set her body aflame with kisses down her neck and over her ears from door to door.

Once home, Kayla dropped the key repeatedly, unable to concentrate as Cole distracted her with repeated, slow, deliberate kisses.

They left a trail of clothing from her doorway to her bed. As if in some sort of erotic time warp, they went from clothed to naked almost instantly.

There was no time to set the mood. No time for the romance of soft music and candles. Need, pure and lustful drove their actions. Kayla threw back the comforter and sheets on her bed before Cole reclaimed her lips to continue his sweet torture.

He blazed a trail down her body until he came to her feminine center. There, he tenderly nipped the soft, silky skin of her inner thigh before parting her folds. Gently, with two fingers, he spread her open. Her sensitized nub throbbed and pulsated from his ministrations.

Kayla breathed in short gulps of air. With excruciating slowness, he went in and out with his fingers, until she thought she would explode, and then he slipped his warm moist tongue inside her.

Waves of ecstasy arced through her. She gyrated her hips to increase the pressure, weaving her hands in Cole's locks to draw him closer.

Powerless to control herself, Kayla screamed out his name as her body released pent-up passion. Attempts at intelligent conversation were futile as she uttered long, surrendering moans. Several minutes later, she still lay panting, her chest heaving from the powerful orgasm.

Voice deep and sexy, Cole said, "Oh no, young lady, that was just the beginning; I've got much more in store for you tonight."

Was it possible to want him so much so soon after such a complete climax? His hardness electrified her. She needed to feel him inside her.

With the patience of an experienced lover, Cole slid his tongue toward her breasts again to continue his loving treatment on each sensitive swollen nipple.

She felt erotic pleasure as he took control of her body. Her lips craved his. And he didn't disappoint with the all-consuming kiss that literally took her breath away. The slow kiss was demanding, insistent and heady with its power. Her body responded without hesitation, as if he'd spoken a command. She arched toward him, her hands playing with the smooth skin of his golden brown chest.

The sound of pleasure echoed off the walls as she gently pulled a tan nipple into her mouth, sending spirals of heat through his body. Her mouth encircled the small bud until it was rock hard. Incredibly, she felt him lengthen in response.

When neither could stand it any longer, he slipped on a condom and entered her...gently teasing her until she was fully ready for him. Together, they found a tempo that bound their bodies together in perfect harmony. What he gave she took and what she gave he took. As he plunged deep inside her, she dug red nails into his back as their fervor reached a feverish pitch.

Kayla lowered her hands to his tight buttocks, scoring them too. She drew him tighter to her; she wanted to feel all of him, and she was ready for his massive expanse—no holds barred.

Passion pounded the blood through her heart, chest and head. He suckled her as he thrust deeper and deeper into her love cavern.

His expert touch sent her to an even higher level of ecstasy as she writhed beneath him.

They moved as one until they climaxed together in an explosion of white light, each crying out the other's name.

Several minutes passed before either could speak or move. They lay satiated and exhausted in each other's arms, their bodies glistening under a smooth sheen of perspiration. Finally, giving into the physical demand for rest, Kayla and Cole slept, bodies intertwined.

In the wee hours of the morning, Kayla awoke dazed and confused to the sensation of her feet being kissed, nibbled and sucked. She gasped in sweet agony. "Hi," she said lazily, stretching her body to give him easier access.

"Hi, yourself, did I wake you?"

"Yes, but that was your intention wasn't it?"

Dangerous Dilemmas

"Yes it was, seems I can't get enough of you, Ms. Williams. What can I possibly do to fix this problem? Any suggestions?"

"Well, give me a few minutes to think about it. I'm sure I can come up with something," she said, giggling.

"Think fast," Cole said as he kissed the bottoms of her feet and moved slowly up her legs. He paused long enough to suckle the fronts and backs of her knees.

Kayla's moans of pleasure aroused Cole even more. His kisses hot and passionate continued to her inner thigh again. Kayla throbbed in anticipation—Cole didn't make her wait long. He slipped his tongue into her now moist folds, thrusting deeper and deeper into her. He gently sucked out her nectar, causing her breathing to come in short gasps. Her chest heaved as he brought her to the brink of completion once again.

The sound of passion came from deep in her throat. Sweat beaded around the edges of her hair. He made her so damned hot.

His eyes smiled at her while his tongue continued its magic at her core. Kayla ran her fingers through his wavy hair as she pulled him closer to her. He plunged his tongue deep inside of her, pulling on her nectar like it was his life's sustenance. He tickled her clit with the underside of his tongue, which heightened the sensation coursing through her. Fire built, threatening to burn right through her.

Seconds later, her body shuddered in a violent climax, and she felt her world shatter into a thousand pieces. Even with her breathing out of control and her body embroiled in deliciously sinful orgasm, Cole was merciless. He inserted two fingers inside her while she came, suckling her at the same time. Kayla thought she would lose her mind. The sensations from all parts of her body sent her spiraling into a realm she never knew existed.

Pleased with himself, Cole watched her panting for air. He was a man who enjoyed satisfying a woman.

When Kayla's breathing slowed down to a normal pace, he continued his sensual assault with more hot kisses down her neck. She was in trouble again, but turnabout was fair play.

46

Deftly, she slid out from under him. She positioned her body to straddle him, giving her more control.

Cole was amused—but pleased. He would let her have her way with him…for a while anyway.

In the same slow torturous manner, Kayla trailed kisses down his neck and across his chest…Her soft hand slid across his abdomen and…

Cole gasped when he felt her warm mouth envelop his testicles. She gently suckled and massaged each lobe, watching him grow to full arousal.

"Come here, woman. What are you trying to do to me?" he barked playfully.

"Just trying to give as good as I get." She smiled down at him, losing herself in the depths of his gold-flecked eyes. *Hmmm…wonder if this is what Tracey means by spreading my wings?* A secret smile crossed her lips. *It's just dinner.*

CHAPTER FIVE

I'd better get every last detail." Tracey crossed her arms over her small bosom while she waited for Kayla to take her first sip of coffee.

Kayla had been late getting to the restaurant this morning, but as her body hummed and buzzed from Cole's all night and all morning lovin', she couldn't complain. And at the moment, she didn't even mind the third degree she received from Tracey. *Now that's good lovin'*, she thought.

"Girl, I'm not telling you all my business. What you need to know is that I...make that we, had a wonderful time. We even have another date planned for tomorrow." For dramatic effect, she tucked a lock of hair back behind her ear before she continued. "Now, if you'll excuse me, I have a lot of work to do. Remember, I have an outside appointment this afternoon."

"Oh my gawd! You did it didn't you? Oh yeah, my girl gave up the cookies. Let Mr. Lewis dip his chocolate in your peanut butter." Tracey did a silly victory dance. "Now, I know you better give up the details. Is he as hung as he looks? Kayla, you are not going to leave me hanging like this. Tell me something, I am so excited for you." She closed her eyes to a squint. "And you used protection right?"

"Tracey, you need a pet! I'll be the first to admit that it has been a while since I've been out on a date, but damn, I'm not a virgin. I know what I'm doing. Like I said, we had a very nice time. Now promise me you won't go trying to pump him for information when he comes in here. Be good." She glared at her friend. "Tracey, I need to hear the words from your mouth."

Pouting, she said, "Okay, damn. But I want to formally register my protest. I've been there for you during all the lonely nights between David and Cole; the least you could do is give me a little dish."

A mischievous grin crossed her lips. "I will tell you that dinner was more than I could ever have dreamed. And the red dress…well, let's just say, I won't be wearing that one again."

"Oh sookie sookie, please tell me he tore the damned thing right off you!"

"Such a flair for the dramatic." *And so close to the truth.* "I'll admit it was a casualty of impatience, but it definitely served its purpose to stir up interest."

Tracey extended her hand to high-five Kayla. "That's my girl. I knew you still had a little slut left in you. So what does this mean? Will Cole become *Mr. Special* for *dinner* on the regular?"

Damn, I hope so. "We've only had one date…A little more time please before you start to plan the wedding."

"Whatever. Just keep me posted. I worked too hard to get you to this point," she joked.

"Back to work nutcase—I've got a meeting this afternoon that I have to get ready for."

12:30 P.M.

Excellent service had been the standard at the diner, but now Cole was treated like a king. Especially after Kayla came to personally take his order. His amused expression comforted her, took the edge off her insecure thoughts. She couldn't be sure that after giving in to physical desire so quickly he wouldn't just disappear. But there he was, looking just as sexy as ever. Again impeccably dressed, the navy blue business suit conformed perfectly to Cole's handsome physique. *And for the moment it's all yours girl.* Kayla pinched herself before she approached him.

"Nice to see you again, Mr. Lewis."

"And you as well, Ms. Williams. I hear the specials are very good at this establishment. But is there anything *else* you'd recommend?"

Kayla tapped her pen against her order pad. "Well, there is something, but as a Tiger, I couldn't possibly serve it to a...*Cock*." She paused for effect.

Desire burned bright in his eyes. "Don't play with fire, young lady. You might be consumed by the flames."

"Promises, promises." With a dramatic shrug, she said, "So I guess you'll have to stick with our stewed beef. I made it with my own two hands this morning, after an especially delightful evening and night."

"Well in that case, I'll order some for now and later. I know what those lovely hands are capable of doing from personal experience. As a matter of fact, I missed them this morning after 5."

Kayla couldn't help herself as she giggled like a schoolgirl. "Perhaps what you need is another *serving*." Kayla's devilish smile lit up her face. Maybe it was Tracey's influence, but she didn't think twice about being so forward. "I should be available at 10:00 P.M. We could have...*dessert*, if you're up to it?"

"I like the way you think, Ms. Williams, especially when you suggest an offer I couldn't possibly resist." Cole thought about all the work he'd neglected the night before. "Would you mind coming over to my place? That way I can finish up everything before you come. I want to give you my *undivided* attention."

"A great idea. I'll take care of everything, just make sure you have an appetite and some energy."

The kitchen was abuzz with energy. Maybelle and Clarabelle gave her a conspiratorial wink before she went back to the floor. *Oh, brother, now Tracey has the Bobsy twins involved too.* Smiling, she thought, *Good thing you're worth it, Mr. Lewis.*

2:30 P.M.

Anxiety gnawed at Kayla's confidence. She pulled into the nearest visitor spot in the bank parking lot, narrowly missing the cement block in front of the space. A million thoughts competed for attention at the same time.

Kayla stared up at the bank marquee. What if this wasn't the right thing to do? What if it didn't go through…then again, what if it did? Mama had always said be careful what you ask for. In this electronic age, the loan application had taken less than fifteen minutes to complete online. But now, this was the moment of truth, she would be talking with a real live person.

If I'm making a mistake, please let me know before I get in there to sign the papers. Kayla gathered her briefcase, which seemed to contain her entire life. She took one nervous step outside the car. Then she remembered something she'd said to Cole about her mother, *she was my champion when I needed her to be.* "Just go in there and do this."

Jacksonville, Florida

Anger flashed in David's dark brown eyes. It was late when he'd driven to Kayla's house, but he knew her schedule front to back. Normally, she would leave the restaurant, drive home and practically pass out after a quick shower. It was this well rehearsed routine that had driven the wedge in their relationship too large to overcome. Their breakup was a little less than friendly, but with the passage of time, he figured maybe it was time to give it another shot.

He took a long drag of his cigarette. Once he withdrew it from his clenched lips, he seemed to study the tip. David was lost in thought, deep, disturbing thought. How could Kayla do this? And why now when he was in the process of relocating from Florida to Columbia, South Carolina. It was time to get his life back on the fast track. A life he anticipated would involve Kayla.

Dangerous Dilemmas

David had spent most of the day with real estate agents, took care of some other business, and then headed back to Hilton Head to surprise Kayla. There was no time to stop by the restaurant so he figured he would see her at home. They would spend some time catching up and then possibly…he would *rub* her tired shoulders. He knew her habits, so there was no need to call ahead. Besides, he wanted to surprise her. *Yeah, but the surprise and the joke are on you buddy.*

David arrived at Kayla's around midnight. At first, when his knocks to the door went unanswered, he figured she was asleep or in the shower…

Out of curiosity, he waited until he was sure she was home. Never did he imagine she would come strolling home at 1:00 A.M. with her luscious lips and body wrapped around some other man. They practically screwed each other on the front stairs. This was ludicrous!

After driving through the night, he sat on the edge of his bed, the only thing he'd yet to pack up. The near-empty room seemed to echo the hollowness he felt in his soul. Even with their breakup, Kayla meant everything to him.

In retrospect, they should never have parted. Sometimes the combination of two strong-willed people didn't work very well. After one too many nights at home alone, he demanded she make a choice—him or the restaurant. A month later, he'd packed his bags.

The Jack and Coke he'd just poured beckoned his lips for another taste. Sleep had eluded him, despite his being fatigued and the numerous glasses of alcohol he'd consumed. His mind kept going back to the same thought—they could have a good life together.

Of course, it would mean she had to agree to give up sole control and responsibility of the restaurant, but they could make it work this go-around as long as she also agreed to give him the time and attention he deserved. He took a long swig of the potent brown liquid.

She was the only woman he'd ever truly loved. And now Kayla Williams, his Kayla, was behaving like a nymphomaniac slut with another man. "I'll be back to reclaim what's mine," he slurred.

Through blurred vision, David looked at the calendar. He still had a few things to clean up before he transitioned to South Carolina, but in a few days, he would make Kayla his top priority. He wasn't ready to give up so easily.

10:00 P.M.

Kayla arrived at the doorstep of Cole's condo with a chilled bottle of Freixenet Sparkling Wine in hand.

With one look at her, he smiled in sultry delight. "Ooh, I like. What are we celebrating?"

Green eyes aglitter, she responded, "It's wine; who needs a reason?"

He barely managed to say another word before he felt her soft supple body press against his and her arms wrap around him. It was the best hello he'd received in a long while. Especially when accompanied by the taste of her warm mouth pressed squarely against his.

"Ummm...welcome to Chez Lewis. I'm glad I had a good lunch earlier, 'cause I have the feeling I'm going to need to be *fortified*."

"Definitely, but somehow, I think you'll be just fine. Something about previous experience leads me to believe that."

"Come here, woman. I want to pick up where we left off. I'll give you the two dollar tour first, and then we can start to work on this wine."

Kayla smiled. *And then I can start to work on you.* "Sounds like a plan. I do have some good news about work, but it can definitely wait until later. Right now, I want all two dollar's worth of my tour."

Kayla smiled as she read the note Cole left on the bed.

Gotta run. I have an early meeting, but I'll call as soon as I'm free. Last night was incredible...not to be greedy, but how about tonight?

Stretching like a feline as she left the bed, Kayla smiled. *Tonight, tomorrow, and the night after that…*

They'd had a lovely time together, and now she felt perfectly lazy. After a quick shower, she went into the kitchen to begin her daily routine. Life wasn't worth living until that first cup of coffee with lots of cream and sugar. She'd slept in 'til 7:00 A.M., but now it was time to get ready to head to the restaurant.

Besides, it felt a little strange to be in his house without him. She would much rather have had Cole at the table with her, but if there was anything that she understood, it was dedication to the job. In the coming weeks, they would both have a lot going on. She with the restaurant and he with the magazine. She noticed he'd left a copy of the latest issue of the magazine with a sticky note attached.

For your reading pleasure.

"I love a man who thinks of everything." She spread strawberry jelly on her toast as she read the upcoming issue of *Full Flava*. She always started her morning off with the business briefs of the Hilton Island Packet to get her in the mood to go to work; however, this morning she read Cole's magazine from front to back. Impressed with the way he put it together—he was a man invested in his product, something she found sexy about him. *Is there anything you don't like about him?*

Kayla picked up her cell phone to dial Tracey's number. She started talking as soon as her friend picked up. "Do me a favor; don't talk, just listen. I'm having a mini-crisis."

"Well, despite your being rude, I'm all ears. What's up, girl?" Tracey replied.

"I spent another night with Cole. It was wonderful, mind-blowing sex. I'm at his house now all by myself because he had a meeting."

"Okay…so what's the problem?"

"Tracey, don't you see? This is terrible. I mean it's wonderful, but it's terrible."

"Will the Martian who stole my friend's brain, please bring it back. We've got work to do."

Kayla huffed. "I told you to shut up. Now, listen. I haven't done this in so long, I'm not sure what to do. Am I moving too fast? Is he making assumptions, just leaving me here to my own devices? I could be the original axe murderer or something. This is so damned comfortable, it is scaring the crap out of me."

"Can I talk now?"

"Yes, smart ass," Kayla responded with a chuckle. "Give it to me straight."

"Thank you, Martian. I'm talking to the real Kayla now. The one who needs to stop being afraid of her own damned shadow. Honey, just enjoy. Why are you complicating everything already? You just said you are having a wonderful time with this man; can't that be enough?" Tracey hesitated as if the light bulb just turned on. "Never mind, don't tell me. You're comparing him to David."

And she scores. "Cole thinks David was one of those relationship-growing experiences for me, but I know better, he was just a mistake— pure and simple."

Tracey chuckled. "Okay, now don't hold back. Tell me how you really feel. I think I agree with Cole. Sometimes you have to go through the pain to figure out what's really important. David served a purpose, but that doesn't mean all the rest of your relationships will turn out the same. Like I said before, just enjoy the moment. I know I would with that gorgeous hunk of man." She paused. "Are you sure you're all right? Is anything else bothering you?"

"I'm not sure." Kayla hesitated. "I don't know. I feel like I'm still looking for something."

"Looking for what?"

Steam rose and swirled above her cup of aromatic fresh coffee before she brought it to her lips for another taste. "Tracey, that's just it. Am I looking for the other shoe to drop? Am I looking for Cole to mess up so I can say, ah ha, you're just like David? He is so wonderful and he makes me feel so good. But, I don't want to be hurt. I suppose I just don't want him to disappoint me like David did, and that's what I have to let go of. It's really not fair for me to make Cole pay for David's mistakes." She was quiet for several seconds as she tried to process exactly what she was thinking. "Does this make me a wuss?"

Tracey laughed. "Nope, just human. Now, will you please bring that juicy butt into work now? Damon and I have plans for this afternoon. Nothing like a little afternoon delight to make up for what we missed last night. Remember I'm off at 3:30 today."

"In that case, *juicy* and I will be there soon. Thanks for the pep talk…" Kayla laughed. "I think. Anyway, I'll be there soon. I have some exciting business news to share with you too."

Tension knotted the muscles deep in his neck as Cole hung up the phone. "Dammit," he said to no one in particular. This little side trip would not only put a crimp in his work schedule, but more importantly, his plans with Kayla. If the meeting in Savannah, Georgia, ran late, he would stay over instead of driving back.

"You've reached the voice mail of Kayla Williams. You know what to do after the beep."

"Hi, darlin'. Just wanted to let you know that something came up with the magazine. I have to run to a meeting to check out some information that's about to go to print. I'll call you as soon as I'm done, but it might be late tonight. Stay at my place if you want. I would love to come home to you…for my own selfish reasons of course."

Pleased at the thought of seeing Kayla again, he returned his attention to the drive. In the space of an instant, Cole looked down to close the phone.

A loud *crash* exploded in his ears, and then everything went blank.

CHAPTER SIX

Kayla's heart pounded in her chest. As the blood rushed toward her head, she fought the feeling to lose consciousness. She'd never fainted in her life, but after Cassandra's call, she was on the verge of it. "What do you mean Cole's in the hospital in Savannah? I just received a voice message from him. What happened?"

"He was in a hit and run accident. From what witnesses say, he was broadsided by a large SUV. Because of the concern for head trauma, he was airlifted to Savannah." Choking back emotion, Cassandra paused. "You're all he's been talking about for days. I know he would have wanted me to call you. I plan to leave in about an hour if you want to ride with me. Frankly, I could use the company."

"Yes, definitely. I'll be ready as soon as you are—just let me know." She tried to keep the panic from her voice as she called Tracey into her office. "Cole was in a car accident in Savannah. His secretary is going to pick me up so we can go there now. I hate to do this to you, but I have to see him."

Tracey's eyes widened with surprise. "Of course you do. Don't worry about us. What did she say about his condition? Is there anything else I can do? Should I go by your house for anything?" Tracey stopped talking before she started rambling. She reached out to hug Kayla, which Kayla gladly accepted as she fought back the tears.

"I don't know too much now, but I'll call as soon as I do. This is unbelievable."

Tracey nodded in understanding. "I know how you feel about car accidents, so get it all out here. You have to be strong for him. He needs to know you're okay; otherwise, he's going to worry about you as much as you worry about him."

Dangerous Dilemmas

As soon as she heard the words *car accident*, she was transported three years back in time. Silent tears fell down her cheeks as Tracey held her. She couldn't lose Cole now.

The drive seemed excruciatingly slow, even though Kayla knew Cassandra was speeding. During the entire journey, conversation had been kept to a minimum. Kayla hadn't even complained about the country music station Cassandra had left on the radio as they drove—something she would normally have teased her about. She would listen to Black Sabbath right now as long as she was distracted from the torture of imagining Cole's injuries.

She closed her eyes to push away negative thoughts. This was not the night her parents died. Not again…tears welled, but she refused to let them fall. Everything was going to be okay. She repeated the words until she began to believe them.

*Inhale…exhale…breathe…*She wouldn't be any good to him if she were a nervous wreck.

It was a beautiful, modern facility, but the sterile, antiseptic odor of Savannah Memorial Hospital threatened to overwhelm her fragile emotions. *Inhale…exhale…breathe…*

They found Robert in the Intensive Care waiting area. Kayla followed Cassandra, who rushed toward him. He wrapped his arms around Cassandra, and then greeted Kayla. "He's out of surgery. He hit his head pretty hard, but luckily, his noggin is so damned hard, they don't think there's any trauma. All the preliminary test results look good. The CT scan shows a serious case of stubborn as hell-it is." Robert hesitated, "But I did have to consent to surgery for him."

Kayla gasped.

"Sweetheart, it's going to be okay." He rubbed her shoulder in a comforting manner. "Maybe from the steering wheel, I don't know, but his spleen was torn during the accident. One of the surgeons indicated he doesn't think it will have to be removed. They're going to try a fairly new procedure to make the repairs with lasers. I know it sounds bad, but I was assured he's very lucky." Robert paused again. "His truck is totaled, and it looks like a semi-truck hit it instead of a sport utility vehicle. So, we should all be very grateful."

Robert could tell from the relieved expressions on both women's faces that at least the most important parts had sunk in—Cole was going to be all right. "He should be coming out of the recovery room and the anesthesia soon. According to the doctors, with this new procedure, he should only have a small war wound, and he could be up and about in a couple of days to a week. But, he shouldn't try to do too much." His gaze settled on Kayla. "Cole is more than welcome to stay with me, but if he prefers to be with you, I'll understand."

Kayla exhaled. The news was better than she'd expected, but she was still terrified. No matter how irrational the thought, hospitals reminded her of death. She didn't think she'd ever get used to being in one. Especially since she'd vowed that after Anke and James died, she would never come to identify the body of a loved one again. A shudder of anxiety passed through her. What Robert said made sense, but it didn't quite quell the feeling of dread in the pit of her stomach.

"Whatever Cole wants, but I have no problem with taking care of him. Thank you, Robert. I feel better knowing you were here for him." She still couldn't believe he'd been in an accident...she need to understand what happened. "Were there any witnesses? Do the police have a license number of the vehicle that hit him?"

"No one has come around to interview me, so I don't know any more than what hospital personnel were told as they brought him in on the ambulance."

"Mr. Lewis is awake now," the doctor said as he entered the waiting area.

Kayla jumped up from her seat. "I have to see him."

The doctor briefly looked down at the chart. "Hello, I'm Dr. Oaks. Are you Kayla Williams?"

"Yes," Kayla said barely above a whisper.

"Good. He's been asking for you since he was brought in from the accident. Before surgery, he was in and out of consciousness, but I'd say you are pretty important to him."

The relief she felt could not be expressed. She had to see him before she exploded. "Thank you, Dr. Oaks. I'd like to see him now."

The doctor smiled at her patiently. "It will be just a few minutes. He's being transferred to a private room now, but I'll have someone come to take you to his ward. In the meantime, relax. The procedure went so well, it might end up in a medical training tape." His disarming smile gave her some comfort. "Trust me, he's doing fine." With that, Dr. Oaks moved on, but he promised to catch up with her a little later to answer any questions she and Cole may have.

A few minutes later, Robert approached her with a cup of freshly brewed coffee. The aroma of which was heavenly, but she was so keyed up she barely tasted it; she just needed something to quench the dryness of her throat.

Finally, after what seemed like an eternity, a nurse came to show her to Cole's room.

Kayla stood at the doorway for a few seconds before she could bring herself to walk into the room. Once inside, she clutched at her heart. He looked so pale, she thought.

Standing next to the bed, she said, "Cole, sweetheart, it's Kayla."

His eyes fluttered open, and he still appeared to be in somewhat of a haze, but as soon as he recognized her, he gave his best attempt at a smile.

Kayla jumped in to assist him as he tried unsuccessfully to raise his head from the pillow. "Don't try to move, I'm right here. Do you need anything, some water?"

"I'm all better now that you are here," he responded in a crackly voice. "I'm sorry for taking you away from your hectic schedule. This was quite a surprise."

She raised her fingers to her lips. "Oh, Cole, don't be silly. I know that it's only been a short time, but I've come to realize nothing in my life means more to me than you. I was so scared after Cassandra called I didn't know what to do. Thank God she drove because I couldn't concentrate to save my soul. I just kept seeing visions of you laying bloodied and hurt, but now look at you — just as handsome and sexy as ever." She gave him a mischievous grin. "Oh well, guess I can go home now."

The color started to return to his gray pallor as he became more alert. "Don't you dare. I need you here with me, woman. Before surgery, the docs said that barring any mishaps, I'd be released either tomorrow or the day after. They want me to take it easy for a week, but after that, I'm good to go. I guess I'll be working from my home office."

Kayla scooted closer to him as she sat down on the edge of the bed. She stroked the side of his face while she spoke softly. "You don't need to think about work at all. Cole, you really scared me. I don't ever want to feel that fear again. I thought my heart would pound right out of my chest." She hesitated. "I'd like to go home with you too, to take care of you during your recuperation. I don't want you bending or reaching for things and aggravating your stitches. I want you to let me take care of you. Promise me you'll let me do that for you."

Cole lifted his body so he could reach out to her. His movements were limited by the constraints of the anesthesia and the dressing. Kayla realized what he was trying to do and put her arms around him gingerly, careful not to apply too much pressure.

She smiled inwardly. As soon as she made contact, she noticed a certain part of his anatomy was more excited than other areas. "Cole Lewis, you are incorrigible."

He gave her a sheepish grin. "Hey, I can't apologize for the effect you have on me. This is exactly the way I like it."

Dr. Oaks found them both chuckling as he walked into the room. "Well, I'm glad you are keeping my patient's spirits up. I've reviewed the chart, and everything looks just fine. We'll keep an eye on you for a couple of days before we make a determination for release. I've ordered some pain relievers for your head and your wound area. Your head made contact with the window hard enough to crack it, but you don't seem any worse for the wear."

Dr. Oaks motioned toward Kayla. "In the meantime, enjoy this beautiful woman here by your side. Let her love you for a couple of days, and you should be ready to return to your *normal* activities no later than two weeks as long as you don't feel lightheaded or dizzy."

The doctor's sly reference to sex wasn't lost on Kayla or Cole.

"You're obviously very important to her." Dr. Oaks patted Cole on the shoulder and with a wink said, "You're a very lucky man."

Kayla looked down in embarrassment as her cheeks flushed with heat.

"Just give a holler if you need anything. I'll be back in the morning."

After the doctor left, Kayla leaned in to give him a quick kiss, which Cole, despite the circumstances, readily accepted. "Before I have to beat you down with a stick, Robert and Cassandra are outside." His quiet chuckle warmed her heart. He was definitely coming around now.

"As much as I'm loving this time with you, I suppose I should meet with them. If for no other reason than to let them know I'm on the mend. But don't go too far. I'm not quite finished with you yet."

Kayla looked down at his hospital gown, which was *raised* in a certain location. "But I'm temporarily finished with you." Kayla wriggled out of his reach. "Mr. Lewis, don't even think about it until you are given medical clearance for *such* activity." If she didn't take steps to cool things down, they just might find themselves in a compromising position. Kayla said, "Besides, we have plenty of time to enjoy each other's company later, like when you're released from the hospital. And just to make sure of your abilities, I plan to play nursemaid for the next few days."

Cole put his hand to his heart. "I'm touched. You're going to neglect the citizenry of Hilton Head just for me?"

"I know. Will wonders never cease? I'm going to owe Tracey big time for taking up my slack, but that's the beauty of working with one of your best friends."

"We'll have to have her and her boyfriend over for dinner or drinks to thank her. Tell her to give you a date."

Mighty comfortable with that 'we' stuff. Kayla smiled. "Yes, boss. Now as for you, maybe I should give you a few minutes before I find Robert and Cassandra."

Cole bunched the blanket over the *tent* he created with his hospital gown. "Problem solved. Now, are you sure I can't get one more kiss before you send in my friends?" His slow seductive dimpled smile left her heart pounding to an erratic beat.

Kayla told herself once more. *Inhale...exhale...*Bandaged and banged up, he still heated her hormones to fever pitch. This was definitely not good. All of a sudden two weeks was looking like a very, very long time. "Cole, I'm going to have the nurse give you stronger meds if you don't behave. I'll be back in a minute."

He tweaked her nose. "You wouldn't dare?"

"Watch me. Now do as you're told. If you play your cards right, you might get a little surprise before I go home tonight."

Robert and Cassandra entered the room as Kayla left. Cassandra rushed over to give him a hug. "Man, you really know how to scare somebody! I didn't think I would make it over the bridge to see you, my knees were shaking so badly."

"I'm fine, really. I'm not quite sure what happened. It seems like a blur right now. I keep trying to put the pieces together, but nothing makes sense. I know I had just left the meeting...and then, I'm just not sure. I remember momentary pain, and that's about it until now."

Robert nodded, concern evident in his worried expression. "Okay, the police are looking into it more. Get some rest now, and I'll check back in with you later. Your vehicle is a total loss, so we'll have to figure out the insurance on it since you were on the job. But enough of that, we'll talk business soon enough—we gotta get you out of here first."

"Thanks for calling Kayla. I appreciate both of you. And don't worry; I'm not going to give y'all a reason to attempt a hostile take over. I'll be back in the office in no time."

Dangerous Dilemmas

The ride home from the restaurant where Cassandra had dropped her off was lonely and miserable, but at least she could take comfort in the fact that Cole was in good hands and on the mend. By the time the three of them left the hospital, he was resting comfortably. Before leaving, Kayla brushed his forehead with a light kiss. *How could such a little devil sleep looking like such a little angel?*

With hospital visiting hours ending at seven, Kayla arrived home close to nine. As she pulled into the driveway, she noticed a large rock, which she stopped the car to move out of the way. As she bent over to move it, a sudden noise made the hairs on the back of her neck stand on end. Every nerve ending screamed for her to take action.

Kayla turned around quickly, ready for battle, but saw nothing. She felt foolish, but she called out anyway. "Is anybody there? Stop playing games. This isn't funny."

The leaves of the bushes at the end of her driveway rustled as two of the neighborhood boys came out dressed in Spiderman and Superman pajamas.

Scared to death by little super heroes. "Bobby and Jojo, what are you two doing up so late?" Kayla's shoulders sank in relief.

Once they realized they were in trouble, the boys looked at each other. "We're sorry, Ms. Williams, we didn't mean to scare you." Eight-year-old Bobby pointed to seven-year-old Jojo. "He wanted some of your good pecan pie. Mom is working late. We're at the house with Jacinda, but she's boring. All she wants to do is watch television and talk on the phone."

The two snickered quietly. "We've been gone for about five minutes, and she hasn't even come to look for us. Then Jojo thought about the pie, so I told him we would knock on your door, but then when you didn't answer we decided to wait in the bushes to see if you were coming home soon. We've been playing hide and seek while we wait. But we were going right back home, we promise."

Okay, okay, nothing like third-grade story telling. Kayla shook her head. It had been a day full of incorrigible males. "Come on you little rascals. It's too late for you guys to be out and to have all this sugar, so I'm going to wrap up some pie for you to eat tomorrow. You boys are in luck. I just happen to have pecan and a peach pie. And I'm going to leave Melissa a note about it so don't even think about trying to be slick."

The expression on their faces brightened considerably at the thought of some of Kayla's sweet confection, though they were visibly disappointed about not being able to eat the pie tonight.

Jojo continued, "We didn't know if you were going to have company. That's why we were waiting in the bushes."

"Well, I'm here and it's just me. So, come on in with me now." Kayla called Jacinda, who was extremely embarrassed about "losing" the kids. She stood at Kayla's door in less time than it took to slice and package the pie.

After shooing the boys out with Jacinda, Kayla cleaned the kitchen. However, without much a mess, it didn't take long to finish. As she wiped the table, she admitted how nice it felt to have little people to look after, even if just for a little bit. The closest she'd come to taking care of children was the rare occasion when she went to her aunt's house to visit with her small cousins. An unfamiliar stirring in her heart gave her pause.

It had been a full day of emotional highs and lows, which her body seemed to be reacting to. Uneasy thoughts vied for attention at the same time, which frayed her nerves to the point of edginess. She felt good, she felt bad…she didn't know how she felt.

Comfort was the goal as she lit several large pumpkin spice candles. Pumpkin was one of the best things she liked about fall weather, aside from the cool down. She put two jar candles at the foot of the steamy tub she'd run and then, after placing a Marion Meadows CD in the player, she lowered her body into the heavenly bubbles.

The emotional drama of the day weighed heavily on her tensed shoulders. Tracey was a good friend, but it was times like these that she really missed her mom. Her resolve slipped a little as she thought about her parents again. Dutch-accented and soft spoken, her mom would help her see everything clearly. Ever her rock…ever her champion.

She and Anke would have talked over coffee and cheesecake or a homemade pie. She would have told her all about Cole, how she was falling headlong for him. Her resolve slipped further. Was there a part of her that could imagine being mom to two little boys who would sit around the table eating hot homemade pie from their grandmother's recipe?

Kayla Williams, what are you doing? Finally, she decided not to fight the battle any longer. She let the tears fall as her body yielded to the emotion she'd tried to contain. Once she was spent, she climbed into her bed to rest. Kayla could accurately identify this newest emotion—*Peace*.

The Crazy Crab Restaurant was one of many good places to eat on the island and a favorite among the local population. It was there that David found Sheila.

"It always amazes me when I see a beautiful woman dining alone."

As she was about to take in a spoonful of She Crab soup, Sheila looked up to see a handsome man who was well built, about six feet tall, with short-cropped hair and a nut-brown complexion staring at her.

Nice eye candy, but so uninvited. She arched a brow. "Can I help you?"

David pulled out the chair beside her and sat. "Maybe we can help each other." He extended his hand in greeting. "I'm David Sutton. Pleased to meet you." He made himself comfortable. "You know, I didn't understand the expression 'the enemy of my enemy is my friend' until now."

"I'm not sure I invited you to sit down, Mr. Sutton. And I'm not sure I want to have this conversation with you. Yet, this is a public place, so feel free to have a seat somewhere else. Any place else that is. Do I make myself clear?"

David smiled. If he weren't otherwise engaged, he might give her a go. The body and weave were working for him.

Never one to be adverse to attention, she had to wonder who this guy was and why he felt he deserved her time. Sheila moved her bowl of soup aside. "Who the hell are you?"

His frank assessment of her continued while he answered. "Your friend...I thought we'd already established that fact. If I'm not mistaken, you want Cole Lewis, which works for me because I want Kayla Williams."

She sat back in her seat. "Okay, you've got my attention. I'll formally introduce myself, Sheila Pickwell." She glanced at her watch. "Start talking."

Gotcha. David leaned back too. "I'm interested in Kayla Williams and you're interested in Cole Lewis. I think we can help each other out. I suspect Kayla will realize the error of her ways faster with a little push from you, if you know what I mean?"

Devilment was clear in her sparkling brown eyes as Sheila smiled mischievously. "And so exactly how did you come to find me?"

"Information is what I do, as they say on television. I work for a Fortune 500 company. I'm not a flake, just someone used to getting what I want. And I don't have that right now, but with your help, I could." David watched for her reaction. He was pleased that she listened so intently. She just might do the trick. "After I saw them together, I made it a point to find out who Cole was. The magazine is how I found out about you. I saw a nice picture of the two of you in *Full Flava*. Must have been at some celebrity function." He knew Sheila's type from one look. The body, hair, nails, make up, and clothes all added up to one thing—high maintenance.

"Interesting. The picture you are referring to was taken last year. Don't you think you took a big gamble?"

"Waking up everyday is a gamble. Besides, I always play to win." The smile that teased his lips never quite reached his eyes. "Sweetheart, this is the information age. With one or two clicks of a button, you can find out a person's entire life story. Tax records show an address, a name and address can lead to a driver's license or bill information. And bill information can lead to credit history, banking, or just about anything else

Dangerous Dilemmas

that can become useful. Once I began, the rest was easy. So here I am. And here you are..." *Five credit cards, to include SAKS and Macy's, Beacon score of 705, address...Sunset Cove.* Inwardly, David smiled. He definitely knew the type.

A waiter came by the table, placing a glass of water in front of David. "Can I get you anything else, ma'am?"

The night Cole threw her out still stung. His rejection prickled around the edges of her delicate ego. If she couldn't have him right now, she would mess up his little game of house. He deserved at least that. Sheila put one perfect, deep plum nail to her mouth in thought. "Yes, you can. Dessert. Something cold...I think I'll have some of your famous chocolate mousse cake."

"And for you, sir?"

David clasped his hands together. "No dessert, but I think I'll have the New York strip— rare."

She raised her glass to him. "To you, David Sutton, a man after my own heart."

"To you, Ms. Pickwell, and the success of our endeavors." David raised his glass. *Clink.* Their new partnership was forged.

CHAPTER SEVEN

Kayla stood at the doorway watching while Robert helped Cole out of the car and to the door—with Cole resisting the attempts of assistance at every turn. Robert was obviously exasperated with Cole for being so obstinate. The discharge orders had warned against too much activity for the next two weeks, advice that Cole apparently had no intention of heeding.

Though she didn't agree with his stubbornness, she had to marvel at Cole's strength. His recovery was sure to be swift if he kept this up. Kayla started to intervene, but then figured they would work it out. Instead, she just enjoyed the show.

"I want to thank you again for agreeing to play nursemaid. I think I might have a little short outfit in my closet for you to dress the part as well."

Kayla looked from Cole to Robert. "See what you can do with him. I'm going to get started on something to eat. Tracey brought over about a month's worth of food from the restaurant. So, I think I'll be able to fatten him up before I send him back to work."

Robert laughed. "Don't do me any favors. He's hard enough to deal with without becoming any more spoiled. I'll let y'all continue to become reacquainted while I call Cassandra at the office to make sure everything's okay."

Kayla looked down at her watch. "Hey, tell her to come over after she's done. We've got plenty of food, and it will be nice to see her again. I have to thank her for getting me to the hospital when I was such a bundle of nerves."

Robert nodded and walked toward the deck to make his call.

As Kayla worked in his gourmet kitchen, Cole was beside himself. He'd spent enough time away from her. He came up behind her to wrap his arms around her waist. "Umm…that smells delicious."

Kayla swatted him with the spoon she was about to use to stir the chicken and dumpling soup. "You do realize I'm responsible for all your food consumption? You'd better be nice to the cook, or she'll give you Brussel sprouts every night. Now, will you please listen to Robert and settle yourself on the couch. I'll be out in a few minutes with your tray. I'm going to have to fatten you up again; I think you lost weight on that hospital food diet." She loved the attention but didn't want him to hurt anything vital. Besides, they had plenty of time for playing around later.

"Don't try to spoil me too much. I might get used to it. I'm going to sit down as you've ordered, but let me know if you need help with anything. Other than a little tenderness to my side, I feel good."

Kayla laughed. "I do this for a living, remember. I'm fine. Now scoot. Just give me two minutes to plate this for you."

Cole chuckled. "I love it when you talk restaurant talk to me. Do it again."

Kayla chuckled as she shook her head. "What am I going to do with you?" She turned back to her work of making sure Cole had a nutritious meal.

After dinner, Cassandra, Robert and Kayla kept him entertained until late in the evening.

"Okay, now back to celebrities. Give me some dirt."

"Hmm, I don't know about dirt, but the magazine will feature quite a few celebrities for the anniversary issue. I was on my way to Savannah to meet with a couple of folks before the accident. I don't print anything until I've confirmed it twice." Cole's smile lit up his entire face, making Kayla smile too. "So far I've confirmed USC's Columbia campus for some of our events. We're going to do a panel for college kids who aspire to write, and I'm going to do a live Letters to the Editor session, which should prove interesting considering the letters I've already received."

Excitement bubbled in the air, and she could tell he was very proud of the events he had planned thus far. "Well, I can't wait—tell me everything."

As he shrugged his shoulders, Cole looked toward Cassandra and Robert. "There's only one way we can share information with you. What do you think, guys, should we let her into the *Flava* club?"

Kayla started toward the kitchen again. Over her shoulder she said, "Did I mention the pecan pie cheesecake, a Kayla specialty, which we have for dessert?"

All three answered, "Oh yeah, she's in."

One week later...

Kayla went through her normal nightly ritual of brushing her teeth and washing her face in the double sink that had kind of become her side, while Cole flossed his teeth on his side of the bathroom.

Then it hit her. She wasn't the same person since Cole entered her life. Nope, she had officially stepped back into *relationship-dom*. She couldn't think of herself as a single woman. They weren't just *booty call* buddies—she felt like Cole's girlfriend...his *woman*.

Wrinkling her nose, she said, "Do you realize how 'couply' we've been acting lately? Friends over, dinner, a movie on the couch? I feel like I've stepped into Mayberry."

Cole took her in his arms. "Yes, and I wouldn't trade it for the world. You've been a real bright spot in my life, Kayla. I thought I was content before you, but now I know I'm happy. And there's only one way I can think of to make this better."

The words filled her like one of his deep, passionate kisses. "And that is?"

"If I could count on you being here with me every day."

Kayla looked away. The little voice that warned her of danger was sounding the alarm loud and clear. She wasn't up for such a major step yet. She needed to get back to the restaurant, resume her life. Besides, what was wrong with their arrangement?

"After I first saw you in the hospital room, I thought I was ready to call the hospital chaplain for a bedside wedding, but I've had a little time to think about it."

Kayla took a deep breath as she collected her thoughts. "I think we've been so hot and heavy practically since we met, that we need to slow it down. I can't imagine another man in my life, but I don't want to do anything hasty. I mean, this is good. I feel wonderful when I'm with you, miss you terribly when we're apart, and I can't say there's anything I don't like."

"Which sounds wonderful, but I hear a *but* coming."

"Cole, I'm going be here until you go back to work, but after that I've decided to go back to my place." She laughed nervously. "You'll probably be sick of me anyway."

"I can be patient. I don't have any doubt you'll be ready to take this to the next level soon enough." He paused as he stroked the side of her face. "If I start to become overbearing, just let me know to back off. I know how to take a hint. Deal?"

She exhaled after several seconds. "Deal. And I thank you for your patience with me. I just want to take it slow. I don't want to have any doubts about us."

Cole took a step backward to lean against the sink. "Has anyone ever told you that you have control issues?"

"I do not!" Her jaw tightened as she spoke.

He favored her with a lopsided grin. "Yes, you do, but that's okay." Cole moved toward her and wrapped his arms around her narrow waist. "So does this taking it slower mean that we can't do this?" Without warning, he brought her lips to his. His touch was more a caress than kiss. The sensation sent spirals of heat between them.

Kayla increased the pressure, as her need for him grew.

He led her out of the bathroom to the bed. Cole felt like he'd been waiting an eternity to hold her again. The headache and pain had all but subsided, not that he cared one bit at this moment. Gently, he eased down onto the bed where he continued his love play, intent on changing her mind about leaving him.

His kisses were velvety smooth and soft as they lit the flame of her desire. Her body reveled in the touch and feel of his caress. She was losing the battle of self-control. "Cole, maybe we shouldn't. Tell me how you feel."

She felt his fingers intertwined in her long hair. "I feel like I want to make love to you, and if you don't kiss me again, I'll explode."

She giggled. "Well, in that case, I'd better do something about that." The fire continued to build between them with each touch, each caress, and each tender kiss. Kayla felt like she was floating down a warm and tingly river of ecstasy. The throbbing at her core began in earnest as his tongue explored her waiting mouth.

She wanted to feel his lips everywhere, from her protruding nipples, which yearned to be free of her clothing, to the pulsating lips of her sex. She wanted him to taste her, licking and teasing until he brought her to the point of no return. Her moans of pleasure mixed with his as she caressed his ever-increasing bulge.

Cole felt his blood turn to liquid desire. He wanted to be inside of her, wanted to hear the southern lilt that he loved as she moaned in cries of release. Cole wanted to pump his sex deep inside of her wet cavern. Long strokes in and out until they both reached their own little part of heaven. He was almost there when he felt her move away.

*Control issues, huh…*Panting she broke away from his embrace. With more conviction than she felt, she said, "Sorry, that's all for now. Doctor's orders, you know. Perhaps you should go to sleep now before you injure something important."

Cole groaned. "You are a sinfully wicked woman."

4:00 A.M.

Back to the grind. Kayla kissed Cole's cheek, knowing anything more would lead to complications. She took a quick shower then headed back to the restaurant.

"Welcome back, boss."

"Thank you, and I owe you big for filling in for me."

Tracey winked. "I know you do. How's Cole doing? Were you a good nursemaid or naughty?"

"He's just fine. On the road to complete recovery. As to your second question, I told you before I wasn't giving up the details. You'll just have to use your very vivid imagination to come up with your own story."

"You never were any fun." She pouted. "Oh well, I'll just have to role play with Damon."

"Yeah, any excuse to jump that poor man's bones. Anyway, as much fun as this is, we've got a lot to cover today." Kayla turned all business as she spoke. She'd put her life on hold for too long, and now this was her time. Guilt would have to take a back seat.

"Last week before the accident, I met with the bank. The loan was approved, so now I have to get cracking on making my plans. This has seemed so far away for so long, but now it's a reality. I know you've seen me with my plans and papers, but the reason that I never shared them is because I wanted to make sure they would become a reality."

"This sounds sort of ominous. What exactly do you have in mind?"

She drew in a deep breath. "You know I loved my parents with all my heart. Right? But I've been unhappy for a few years about the way things are around here. I love this restaurant, and I love this community, but I'm not invested in this diner style any more. I want to feel passionate about what we do on a daily basis. We see the same folks, make our product the 'old' way." She waved her arms in a gesture that had become synonymous with Vanna White. "I'm still using the first computer my father ever bought. It's as if we're stuck in this time warp...so much so that my running the diner has gone from a labor of love to a job." Her voice filled with emotion. "This was what they loved. I want to love it again too. I want to turn this space into an upscale bistro and grille."

"Oh my gawd, Kayla, are you crazy? How could you even think of destroying what your parents started here? This place is an every Sunday treat for a lot of families in the area. Please don't frou-frou it up! That's all we need, another eatery serving pretty food that will have you glowing in the dark in ten years. Kayla, we serve the real deal here, think about it, honey."

So much for being able to count on my best friend. "Tracey, I've done nothing but think about it. Every day, I come in here and something else is broken, or I think about the fact that it takes two people to mix up pancakes for Sunday brunch or that I am in here every night doing paperwork as if I lived in a third world country." Kayla sighed. "I understand the way you feel, and I'm sure if I asked others, they would agree, but I can't do this." Her voice dropped to a whisper. "Not anymore. I need my own life, need my own damned identity."

Tracey was silent as she listened. A first for her, but Kayla could no longer worry about public opinion. She'd already made up her mind.

"Anyway, we can continue this later. I need to get to work." She spread the papers on the table then walked out to greet the customers.

The rest of the day went fairly well, save for the bitter feelings her conversation with Tracey stirred up.

Toward the end of the evening, tired of being cooped up in her office, Kayla went back to circle the crowd again. She was delighted to see that business was brisk as tourists and locals headed into the diner for an early dinner.

"So what's good here?"

A voice she recognized but hadn't heard in a while sounded from behind her. Kayla's breath caught in her throat. "David? What are you doing here?"

CHAPTER EIGHT

S
ince I'm moving back into the area, I thought I'd come by to see you." His brown eyes sparkled in open assessment. "It's been awhile…you look great."

Suddenly, she had the urge to cover up. David's glare made her feel naked. "Well, you'll always know where I am, not much has changed. Would you like to order?" *Or maybe just get the hell out?* "There's plenty on the menu to fill you up for your *journey*."

Chuckling from her not so subtle innuendo, David sat back in his chair. "Surprise me, bring me something you'd recommend. How about something you'd like for me to *eat*."

Kayla placed a hand on her hip. "Be right back with your fried chicken livers—house specialty."

The rumble of his laughter rang in her ears as she walked away. *What the hell is he doing here?* Mother always said to trust your gut instincts, and right now, they were screaming at her to do something about him. The problem was…what? As far as anyone else was concerned, he was just another patron. The only *crime* he'd committed was to come to the diner and enjoy the food. Unfortunately, that wasn't going to wash with law enforcement.

David sat in the diner for the better part of two hours. In addition to his meal, he ordered coffee and pie. He ate with relish and sent his compliments to the chef several times. Outwardly, it appeared innocent, but all the while, he watched Kayla and occasionally Tracey like a lion stalking his prey.

A slight shudder of anxiety coursed through Kayla as she watched him leave. This wasn't the end, no matter how much she wanted never to see his face again. David didn't do anything half way, and he never did something without an ulterior motive.

Tracey came to the door and stood with her as he pulled off. "What a day, huh?"

Kayla nodded her head. "Yep."

"I'm sorry about jumping all over you earlier. I know it's not really my business. I just work here. This is about your family, and you have to do what's right. I'm sure being an only child created quite a burden for you."

"Don't worry about it, right now. I can't think about what I want to do. I plan to make a formal presentation to the staff soon, but for now let's just get ready to leave. I think I've had enough emotional upheaval for one day." Kayla rubbed her arms. *Whatever your plan is, David Sutton, just make sure it doesn't include me.*

Unable to dismiss unpleasant thoughts of her previous relationship, Kayla decided to be more cautious driving to Cole's house. The convoluted route she ended up taking made her feel a little more comfortable that David wouldn't know where she was. She did not intend to have him wait for her outside Cole's house every night.

By the time she made it to bed, she had a headache. For the first time in their burgeoning relationship, Kayla didn't want to be touched—she just wanted to be left alone. Cole respected her decision and scooted over to his side of the bed.

Tension built in her neck and shoulder muscles, knotting them together in painful twists. It was one hell of a miserable night, but she couldn't bring herself to talk about David's reappearance just yet. Not while the wound felt open and exposed. Kayla kept it bottled up as she wiped away silent tears. Finally, she gave in to exhaustion in the early morning hours.

In the morning, before she was ready to walk out the door to the diner again, Cole made her coffee and toast. He never asked her what was wrong, just treated her with love and patience.

Dangerous Dilemmas

On edge and sleep deprived, she drove back to work. As she pulled into her owner's parking space, the realization hit her like crash dummies into a wall—full force with no brakes. She loved Cole. No holds barred, she had fallen for him, utterly and completely. Kayla rested her head on the steering wheel. *Oh gawd, what the hell do I do now?*

Two weeks later…

The dark, smoke-filled bar had always been one of their favorite places to relax, especially after his first day back to work. *Island Rhythms* had been a part of local culture for decades but after all this time was still little more than a shack. The bar had three televisions, each apparently permanently positioned on one of the ESPN stations.

However, it was a shack that served the best chili fries in town and made great drinks for a low price. Off the beaten path, it survived with the support of faithful locals, those with a cast iron stomach and a good story to tell.

Full Flava Magazine purchased many a story from the town's folk who frequented the establishment. Cole and Robert sat at their usual table drinking and winding down. Only this time, Cole wasn't drinking anything stronger than a cola with a shot of flavoring in it.

It was something they hadn't done in a while, Robert reminded Cole as he ribbed him in a good-natured way. "So, Kayla let you out tonight?"

Cole smirked. "Don't hate. I'm only hanging out with you for an hour. Kayla should be getting home around the same time I do." He took off his jacket and loosened his tie, soaking up the casual atmosphere in the process.

Robert laughed. "I'm not hatin'. I'm glad for you. I've seen a nice change in you. Since you've been getting 'regular lovin,' you seem much happier. Of course, now this means you'll probably be taking more time off and wanting more money."

Cole nodded in agreement. "That's right. I'm going to have to start playing the relationship card. I can't stay late because my woman wants me at home with her. And of course, once we start having kids, I'll have to take full advantage of the Family Medical Leave Act. Yep, twelve weeks per baby, and I figure we'll have three in three years."

Robert looked horrified.

Bursting at the seams with laughter, Cole clapped Robert on the back. "Man, what's gotten into you? I'm not serious. I haven't even popped the question yet."

Robert almost choked on the deep swig he'd taken of his Hefeweisen beer. "Damn, I know you didn't just say *marriage*."

"I'm just waiting for the right time." Cole took another sip of his coke. "I'm not getting any younger. The magazine is doing well, and life seems to be going well. This seems like the time to make that kind of move. If not now, then when? I think Kayla is perfect for me. We have the best relationship I've ever had with a woman. I think she understands me; besides, she's good for me. I feel settled when we're together. And I'm ready to have that all the time, not just on certain days or strictly on weekends. I want her in my life twenty-four seven."

"Nice…" He looked at Cole in earnest. "So, how does Kayla feel?"

Cole looked up momentarily at the television mounted in front of the bar. The classic channel was showing a Mike Tyson marathon. He gave the TV a cursory glance before he turned his attention back toward Robert. "I think she feels the same way, but she's playing it safe." He shrugged. "I guess it's my job to make her feel more secure. She had a bad break up with her last boyfriend. Unfortunately, while she's over him, she's not over the trauma of betrayal." Cole paused. "She hasn't said too much, but from what I can tell, it wasn't good. I think he did a number on her. Kayla tells me more with her silence. David is someone I'd like to meet in a dark alley…only one of us would make it out. But as far as Kayla's feelings about me, I've got the feeling I have a little more work to do. With a little more time, we'll get there."

"Does this have anything to do with the accident? I've heard of folks jumping into commitment because they think they're going to die before too long. I like Kayla, don't get me wrong. She treats you right, and the girl can throw down in a kitchen, but are you sure?"

"Never more in my life. I know I made a mistake with Sheila. I should have let her go before she became too attached. We were both kicking it, and she knew that, but somewhere along the way, she figured I was her meal ticket. And I won't complain, 'cause we had fun, but she just doesn't know when to quit."

Robert raised his glass. "Amen to that. One of these days she'll learn her lesson."

With a smirk, Cole added, "So when are you going to make an honest woman out of Cassandra? I know you two are kicking it hard. Having that little office romance thing going."

After a long sip, Robert finally said, "There's nothing much going on. We enjoy each other's company…she told me she doesn't want anything serious. And to be honest, I'm fine where we are. It's monogamous; it's fun. She's laid back, giving, and knows how to pull back when it's time. Sometimes we go days without doing more than seeing each other at work, and she's cool with that. For right now, she's everything that I want and need."

Cole nodded. "That's good, just make sure that if the relationship changes, you two work it out. We've got enough drama as it is," he teased lightly.

Robert raised his glass of beer. "Amen to that too. Keep me posted about lovely Ms. Williams. I guess I'll either be the best man or the pall bearer—depending on how you look at it."

"Best man, so get used to it. You'll be the second person to know when I pop the question."

Cole returned to find Kayla's packed bags by the door. "Kayla, you know you don't have to do this? I love having you here with me, and there's plenty of room for you to bring over more of your things. You're not relegated to only a few clothes and your toothbrush."

She nodded her head as she smiled. "Yes, I know. And believe me, I have loved every minute of being here with you as well, but I have to stick to my word. Besides, I'll be back next weekend. But for now, I think we need to maintain our own space. It'll be better for us in the long run."

Cole laid his suit jacket over the edge of the seat as he made himself more comfortable. "Remember what I said about spoiling me? I've really enjoyed waking up to you and going to bed with you by my side. I'm not so sure I'm ready to give that up yet." He wanted to touch her, feel her in his arms as he had been all week, but they needed to talk.

Kayla turned her lips up to a lopsided grin. "Although you've made it extremely difficult for me to want to do this, I'm going to stick to my plan. I've grown accustomed to playing our own little game of house too, but this is bigger than just about our pleasure." She paused. "Okay, I'll admit it. I'm really going to miss the pleasure part, but I refuse to give in to my carnal, lustful desires when it may go against the greater good."

Cole smirked. "Since when is going against one's carnal, lustful desires ever a good thing?" To punctuate his point of view, Cole took her into his arms for a deep, knee-shaking kiss.

After she finally broke away from his lips, she desperately wanted to change her mind and promise him she would never leave his side. But her resolve remained strong. Instead, she gave a deep, satisfied sigh.

"Come on. I have dinner waiting. And don't think of it as a Last Supper. It's just a little something I threw together. In case you hadn't noticed, I've made you my little guinea pig since you were kind of my captive audience. This whole week I've been working on recipes I want to add to the menu."

"So what's on the menu for tonight? It smells full of flavor and delicious! Being the food connoisseur that I am, I think I detected a hint of rosemary when I came through the door."

Kayla was impressed. "Good nose. I'm making Chicken Cacciatore. I want to serve it during our annual International Week at the restaurant.

After some macaroni and cheese, potato salad, collard greens, and ham—nothing says comfort more than a big bowl or plate of Italian."

Cole grinned. "And you call me a nut."

"Cacciatore requires a lot of fresh ingredients, so I think it will go over well with our customers."

Cole nodded in agreement. "If it tastes half as good as the aroma, you've got an instant hit. Let me go wash up, and then I'll help out."

He set the table and then selected a nice Portuguese Madeira to go with the chicken. Its rich flavor would complement the dish perfectly. As a fortified wine, the alcohol content would be much stronger, but would still mix well with the spicy flavors of the dish. He would have to stick to half a glass for the evening.

After dinner, they relaxed together on his couch in front of the television, which had become a part of their nightly routine together.

Kayla felt pretty good, after her third glass of Madeira. She sat between his legs as Cole leaned back into the deep, plush leather sofa. She felt the rhythmic beat of his heart against her back and the rise and fall of his chest as he breathed in and out. She loved the bass-filled rumble deep in his chest as he laughed at Maxine's antics on the show "Livin' Single."

And you want to give this up, why?

"I need to be honest about something." Kayla met his gaze headlong. "It's nothing bad so put your guard down. I've just been trying to sort out my feelings about a recent incident. David came in a couple of weeks ago. He ordered lunch, said a few words, then left. I wanted to tell you so you wouldn't think I'm holding back from you. Also, because I still find him to be somewhat disturbing. I don't want to seem like one of those hysterical women from a horror movie, but seeing him bothered me. Even though I can't concretely put my finger on the reason why."

"Well, what exactly did he say?"

"Nothing really. Like I said, he ordered, ate, hung around for a bit, and then left. I know I sound crazy, so I'm just going to shut up now." *How do you explain that your ex-boyfriend gives you the creeps for no good reason?* "I don't even know why I brought him up, especially at this point.

He said he was moving to Columbia. I don't even know if he plans to come back to Hilton Head or not. I think he was just passing through, and I suppose I was a stop on the way."

"I doubt that seriously. No man in his right mind would make you a pit stop. But as a man, I know he didn't just stop in to say hi. That's a woman thing. He came in because he wanted you to know he was back...he was feeling you out." Cole rubbed her shoulders in an affectionate gesture. "Would you mind telling me what went wrong in your relationship? If it makes you uncomfortable, you can just forget I asked."

Hmm...he's a maniac. Kayla leaned into his embrace. "David is the kind of guy who is handsome and charming and wonderful in the beginning. He sort of gets you where he wants you, and then bam! I'm not saying he has two personalities, but he's a manipulator. While we were together, he was the perfect boyfriend: kind, considerate and giving. Then one day, I looked up and realized it was all a lie. I had been sucked into this vicious whirlpool."

"What do you mean?"

"It's hard to explain because it's more emotional than tangible. David liked what David liked, and he wanted what he wanted. So if that meant I had to give up everything to be his ideal, that's just what it meant in his eyes. There was a point where I felt unless I catered to him, I should feel guilty. I don't know if I'm explaining this correctly or not. He was toxic to me...he was my 'Bobby Brown' so to speak."

Kayla reached for his hand. Her kiss to his palm was a feather light caress. She wanted him to know how much his gentleness meant to her before she continued. "David was never physically abusive or threatening, but he was just as dangerous. He seems to understand your weak spots, and like a boxer, he just pounds away until you're down for the count. We broke up when I stood up to him. But it wasn't easy, and the thought of being in another relationship like that terrifies me. I don't know if I'm strong enough to walk away again."

"You don't ever have to worry about that with me. I'm in your corner. If I need to do a little wall-to-wall counseling with David, just let me know. It can be easily arranged."

Dangerous Dilemmas

Kayla wasn't sure she liked Cole's sudden icy tone. She wasn't trying to upset him, just make him aware in case they happened to run into each other again. At least that's what she tried to convince herself she was doing. At the moment, it just felt like she was being a wuss, something she despised in herself. *Shake it off, girl.* "Well, let's just forget about him. If he comes around again, I'll be sure to let you know. I'd rather focus on us right now and not anyone else in the world."

She kissed his palm again, this time kicking it up an erotic notch by kissing along his fingers. Then she began to suck each one in long pleasurable strokes in her warm moist mouth.

"Hmm, that feels good. Let me see if I can come up with a little something to distract you from any further unpleasant thoughts."

Cole brought her to him as he kissed her long and deep. He crushed her full lips to his own, intensifying the feelings of pleasure. Heat swirled from unknown places, making her head spin in giddy ecstasy. By the time he was finished with her, she couldn't even spell David.

"Yeah, that works," she sighed.

Even half a glass of the potent wine was enough to put Cole in a good mood. He began to stroke Kayla's breasts through the thin fabric of her top. He reveled in their instant response.

Their kisses were gentle at first. After all, Cole was still on the mend. Heat from their contact threatened to scorch the couch they sat on. Cole's erection nearly burst through the front of his slacks.

Throwing caution to the wind, Kayla began to stroke him. He moaned in response, which gave her all the encouragement she needed to continue. Cole drove his tongue deeper into the sweetness of her mouth, acting like a man who couldn't get enough of her.

Damn, she wanted him. *Three weeks is long enough…besides, Dr. Oaks said when we were ready, and damn, I'm ready now.*

She had to hope they could take it slow enough not to put him back in the hospital as she broke the kiss long enough to unzip his pants. His hard penis sprung into view. Kayla wet her lips. Her hot mouth was on him, licking up and down slowly with her tongue. An expert now at giving him pleasure, she swirled his head around in her mouth, listening to his moans of appreciation while she did. Kayla nipped at his sensitized member with her teeth, causing him to shiver in anticipation.

He tried to pleasure her with his fingers, but she shooed him away. When it was time for them to be together, he could bring her to climax anyway that he wanted—but right now it was about him. After several minutes, his breathing returned to normal. "You are a wonderfully wicked young woman."

Kayla smiled. "Thank you. I do my best."

He dipped his head low to capture her lips in his. His tongue explored her sweetness, as his kiss became more passionate. Kayla found herself responding in a most sensual way. She enjoyed the feeling of their tongues intertwined until the wetness and throbbing between her legs became uncomfortable. Her body, acting on a will of its own, closed the distance between her and Cole. Her back arched to feel more of him.

Cole caressed the small of her back, absently tracing the petals of her rose tattoo as he lifted the edge of her top for better access. The heat from his hand seared a path of desire along her skin.

Unlike before, tonight he intended to finish what he started. He pulled Kayla into his arms to kiss the hollow of her neck, all the while he caressed the rounded flesh of her breasts.

Kayla felt distinctly overdressed. She removed her top and bra before she moved his hands back where they felt the best. He stroked her breasts, bringing her nipples to life. But he didn't stop there. His greedy mouth alternated kisses between her mouth and her breasts.

Her heart pounded in her chest as he continued to bring her to higher heights. Cole spread the sofa cushions on the floor then gently lowered her down. He was losing his patience, but he wanted to go slow for her. His lips continued to explore the soft, gently bronzed skin from her breasts to the soft hair of her center. Languidly his mouth and tongue caressed the pulsing bud between her thighs. Kayla bucked toward him, pulling his head for a better taste.

Sensing her need and impatience, he thrust his tongue deep inside, laving her walls and clit to erotic perfection. He wasn't satisfied until she writhed on the cushions, muttering unintelligible sounds of delight.

Close to completion, she quickly shifted her position to be on top. Cole took the opportunity to completely undress then took a condom out of his pants pocket. He wanted to see her face when she came so he helped her down over his waiting throbbing member. Kayla was a vision, earthy, natural and dazzling. Her hair grazed the tops of her breasts creating an erotic picture for him to behold. Cole squeezed each nipple between his fingers until they were swollen peaks and Kayla moaned in appreciation.

The rest of the world ceased to exist as the only sound she heard was the sound her heart threatening to beat straight out of her chest. Each touch brought a quivering response. She needed him—now. Once Cole protected them, she moved over him, taking him into her folds inch by delicious, hard, swollen inch. She continued her movements with intensity and fervor, demanding that he give her everything he had.

The fire between them grew stronger, the flames licking the edge of consciousness. Nothing else existed beyond heated desire at this moment. "Right there baby," she growled. "Oh gawd, right there, baby. I'm coming."

He grabbed her hips, pulling her to him, matching her stroke for long stroke until his quiver of release matched hers and they both gave into the fiery explosion of climax.

Sweat dampened and exhausted, neither one moved until the supernova of explosion ceased.

Hours later, they stood at Cole's door about to say good-bye.

Reluctantly, Cole let her go. "Thank you for being such an excellent nursemaid. Hopefully, I won't have to get into another accident for you to wear that cute little nurse's costume I have hanging in my closet."

Kayla giggled. "Good night, my incorrigible patient."

The drive should have been a simple, twenty-minute affair. But the closer she made it to her place, the more hesitant she became. Maybe she should have taken Cole up on his offer to drive with her. *This is ridiculous. This is home; why am I acting like such a baby?*

Several times she wanted to turn the car around, but she didn't. Finally, weary from the emotional battle she'd waged with herself, she was standing on her own doorstep about to enter her house. Funny how now it felt like much less of a home.

As soon as she entered the house, she thoroughly checked each room. She felt as if she were doing a bad impression of a cop show, sneaking up to each door and slowly opening it. By the time she made it through the house, she felt better because she didn't find anything immediately amiss after not being there for a while. Was it being security conscious or was it paranoia? Maybe a little of both, she decided. Her mother had advised her to get an alarm system, but she hadn't taken the time to order it yet. Oddly, this was the first time she regretted that decision.

Kayla settled in for the night, fighting with herself over whether to jump back into her vehicle and race at break neck speed back to Cole's place.

David watched her go in. A quick study of human nature, he came to a conclusion. *A little spooked, huh? Wonder why that is, Ms. Williams?* He took comfort in the fact that he'd been able to get a reaction from her at all. It let him know that Cole wasn't a serious threat. If she reacted...she cared. And that's all he would need in order to get her back.

As he drove away, the raspy voice of Anthony Hamilton played on his radio. *How appropriate,* he thought as he heard, "No matter what the people say, I'm gonna love you anyway. I can't let go..." He sang along boldly with one person in his thoughts. "Soon, Kayla, soon," he said.

Dangerous Dilemmas

After a disappointing night without Kayla in his bed, Cole made it into work early. He sat at his desk, knee-deep in work when Robert came to his office.

"Pack your bags, bro. Looks like we have a major story to write up. I know you've been through a lot lately, but you're the only one who can pull this off," Robert said. "Cassandra booked a room at the trendy new Twelve Hotel & Residences where you'll be staying in a deluxe one-bedroom suite for three days. I've heard the rooms are all that and then some, so we expect a full report. It's off to the ATL for you. You're meeting with one of the hottest groups in the country."

Robert always did have a flair for the dramatic, but Cole's natural curiosity got the best of him. Being on the hunt for a good story or pulling off the exclusive of the year always pumped his adrenaline. Cole leaned back in his chair while he put his feet up on his mahogany desk.

"Okay, I'm biting. What have you and our beautiful young assistant cooked up now?"

Robert patted himself on the back then sat down in one of Cole's burgundy, leather office chairs. "Thanks in part to my superb networking, you're going to help *Full Flava* scoop all magazines with this story. You know in Atlanta they make it do what it do with a little southern charm. It's going to be hot."

The meeting with Robert to solidify all the details lasted another hour. Cole had just enough time to run home to get himself together before his flight.

Cole checked his watch and noticed it was still fairly early in the morning. He decided to call Kayla from the airport. After their last conversation about David, he didn't want to spend any time away from her, let alone three long days. More than ever, he wished she had stayed at his place. At least there he would have known she was all right.

The announcement about his flight roused him from his musings. The new security protocols made travel a major ordeal. He made it just in time to check his luggage for his flight. Unable to get a good signal on his cell phone, he'd intended to use a pay phone to let Kayla know of his travel plans, but a last minute change in the gates had him running through the airport like an old O.J. commercial...and given the climate of increased security consciousness, that was not cool.

It was fair to say, he was more than a little pissed off by the time he took his seat in first class. As soon as he was settled, he took out his phone again. *Network failed.* Cole wanted to throw the damned thing out the window.

Cole swirled his cognac and coke. The drink reminded him of their first date at *The Blue Note.* So much had happened since then, yet he wasn't where he wanted to be with the relationship. *How long will you put me off, Kayla?* He shook his head. Decision made...his patience had just run out. It was time to take control. He took another sip of his drink as he contemplated his next move.

Smooth, sweet, sexy. His body reacted to the thought of the first time they shared cognac. Images of the first time they made love danced in his memory. He came to the conclusion that even a first class seat wasn't the best place for erotic fantasizing.

Nonetheless, he thought of the first time he saw her beautiful body naked and the first time his hands caressed her soft, supple skin. Cole took another drink. The smoothness of the "yak" reminded him of her taste, her essence, her feel as he dipped his tongue deep inside her femininity. *Damn.* It should be illegal for a woman to be able to do this by the mere thought of her.

The flight attendant had to repeat herself to wake him from his daydreaming. "Sir, is there anything I can bring you?"

Her bright smile was full of promise. Cole took a moment to appreciate the attractive woman with the mischievous twinkling blue-green eyes. She was beautiful in the classic sense—fair complexion surrounded by wavy, thick brunette hair, which she wore styled to frame her face. "Ahem." He cleared his throat. "I think I'm fine for now, but thank you."

The flight attendant leaned in closer as she gave him a pillow to place behind his head, during the course of which Cole had a more direct view of her firm, full C-cup breasts.

Cole licked his lips as Kayla came to mind. Her breasts fit perfectly in his hands, and he couldn't wait to…He stopped his train of thought. He didn't want the flight attendant to think he was lusting for her.

Cole breathed a silent sigh of relief when she moved on to the other male passenger in first class. He had to smile to himself as he watched her perform the exact same routine with the other guy.

Thankfully, a few minutes later, the captain indicated it was safe to turn on electronic devices. Cole finished the drink then inhaled a deep breath. He exhaled after a few seconds. He repeated the process until he felt centered. Then he took out his laptop and pressed the power button. During the process, he ignored the hard-on that pressed uncomfortably between his legs.

He stopped thinking about Kayla long enough to think about upcoming business opportunities. Eventually, his full concentration was on his work. He would ask all the standard inquiries, but also some of the more in-depth questions that had become synonymous with the *Full Flava* style. He could barely contain his excitement, but only after the issue was on the stands would he celebrate.

A tapping sound on the tree near her window and the serenade of several birds woke Kayla up. It was odd to be back after becoming so comfortable with Cole in his home.

If she was to be honest with herself, after adding a few of her personal touches, his condominium felt like a joint domicile. Cole had never made her feel like a guest or intruder. She'd even moved a few things around. It was dangerous when a woman started to rearrange a man's living quarters—definite signs that things were moving beyond the casual friendship. Especially since Cole seemed to appreciate each change.

Kayla smiled as she began to sort through a few laundry items she hadn't completed while at his place. She put away some of her cleaned and pressed clothes, absently humming as she did. In less than an hour, her house was back to normal. She went back to the kitchen to fix a quick bite to eat. Then she noticed it. A small envelope stuck between the napkins in her napkin holder...subtle, but not totally inconspicuous. Kayla's hand shook as it moved toward the manila envelope. Prickly fear wormed its way through her body before shattering her self-control. As realization settled in her mind, Kayla felt like she couldn't breathe. *Someone had been in her house.*

CHAPTER NINE

Adrenaline pumped through her veins, forcing her body to perform an action her head told her not to do. She sat down at the same time she grasped the offending thin paper between nervous fingers. Kayla peered inside to see what the intruder had left for her.

She nearly jumped out of her skin. *David…Dammit. Back in town and back to his old tricks.* This was a message to show her he'd been back in the house…her house.

Tension started to build at the base of her neck. Why did he have to come back now when she was finally happy with someone else? He needed to slink back to wherever he came from and leave her alone. Things would never be different between them, no matter how much she wanted to let go of old feelings of hurt. At the restaurant, David looked nice, said nice things, but he was still the same David Sutton who'd made her life miserable before they broke up. He was still a devil in sheep's clothing.

Damn you, she thought. She held her hands to her mouth and choked back the tears that sprang to her eyes. She couldn't allow herself to be transported back in time to when he'd made her feel alone and vulnerable. Her life was different now. She was different now. *Not this time.*

Before she confronted him, she wanted to talk with Cole. *Don't let him have this power over you*, she told herself as she dialed.

Dammit! Cole's direct line went straight to his voice mail. Next, she called his office.

Cassandra said, "I'm sorry Kayla. He was called away suddenly; he's in Atlanta. He should be at the hotel right about now, according to his travel itinerary, if you'd like that number?"

A stab of disappointment jolted her back to reality. *What is Cassandra saying?* She wasn't clocking his every move, but it wasn't too much to expect to know when he left South Carolina. "No, I'll wait for him to call, thanks." Did she have the right to expect more from him? Was she projecting her relationship ideal on him? Maybe it wasn't his plan to call until he was on his way back home. Then what? Would she act like a possessive girlfriend?

Cole Lewis, there best be a damn good reason why I haven't heard from you.

Kayla looked down again. Tension and anxiety dueled for control over her heart. It was just a picture, she tried to tell herself. With unsteady hands, she took the photo out again to study it…to remember what she'd tried so hard to forget during these months without David in her life. That day came back in vivid detail.

There she was standing next to David, both dressed to the nines looking like the happiest couple on earth. They had attended a business function for him, a promotion from assistant director to director of the bank's information technology department.

Kayla had been proud of his accomplishments until she realized the cost, recognized his ruthlessness. That promotion day, her blood had run cold as he talked about his plans to continue moving through the ranks. David walked *on* the bones, forget climbing over everyone to get to the top; he wanted to annihilate the competition. Anyone in his way became the enemy. It didn't matter who or what got in his way. He was obsessed with winning.

Love, honor and obey…David's own personal commandments.

She'd stood there in the red dress he'd bought and insisted she wear, looking the part of the perfect girlfriend. All the while, she'd felt like she was dying inside. Bile rose up in her throat.

Kayla hated the picture and everything it represented. The endgame was control and humiliation. *Not this time, David, not this time.* This go round, she wasn't fighting alone. At least she prayed not. She closed her eyes. "Cole, please call me."

As soon as Cole was settled, he called Kayla, intent on apologizing for being out of the loop.

She answered on the first ring. "Oh, thank, God. Where are you?"

"What's the matter, sweetheart? What's happened?"

Inhale...exhale...breathe...think before you speak. "I'm just a little spooked that's all. Remember we agreed that I would tell you if I saw David again. Well, he's definitely made contact with me. I'm a little shaken up that he came to my house, but I'm doing better now."

"What do you mean, he was at your house?"

"Calm down, Cole. I didn't mean to upset you. I never changed my locks from before, so he must have let himself in. He left an old photo of the two of us on my kitchen table. It was a message."

"You damn right it was. I think it's about time I left him one of my own. Did he tell you where he was staying?"

"No, and even if he had, I don't think I would tell you. I'm not going to have some Neanderthal boxing match going on. Just let me handle him. If I need to, I'll go to the police later. But for right now, he hasn't done anything but show up again. He's making a nuisance of himself and invading my space."

In truth, she was just this side of scared shitless, but there was nothing Cole could do about David from Atlanta. A laugh so nervous it sounded hollow to her own ears escaped her lips. "So tell me about Hotlanta."

"Kayla, don't put on a front for me. I can change my plans and be on the next flight out. I don't want this guy to think he can walk all over you. Not when I'm in the picture." Cole paused, and she could hear the long breath he expelled. "Kayla, I love you."

With her emotions on the verge of collapse, those should have been welcome words, but she couldn't handle them right now. *Inhale...exhale...breathe...* The walls felt like they were closing in on her. "Cole, for me, don't say things like that, please," she whispered.

Silence filled the space between them. Kayla's heart beat a slow, uneasy rhythm.

Finally, he said, "Promise to call me if something else happens. I need to have your word on that. I don't even want to think about that bastard doing something to you."

You are such a coward. Kayla exhaled. Why couldn't she tell him she loved him back? "I'm fine, but thank you for wanting to be my knight in shining armor." She paused as she struggled for control.

Once she felt better, she said, "Okay, now, tell me why I didn't hear from you? And just so you know before you begin, there is no good excuse."

The view of the Atlanta skyline was breathtaking. Cole thought the only way to make it perfect was if Kayla were there in his arms. He hoped he hadn't put her off with his profession of love. He was a patient man, he could wait for her to realize how much she loved him, but he wouldn't wait for David to do something to her. He kept those thoughts to himself, however, because Kayla had made her point. He didn't intend on having any boxing matches, but he sure as hell would protect the woman he loved.

"I know I'm in trouble. It was a comedy of errors, and you're right, I should have found a way to call you. If I promise never to do it again and agree to fulfill your most outlandish sexual fantasy, will you forgive me?"

"Damn, you're smooth."

He lowered his voice to a seductive whisper, "I'll take that as a yes."

The suggestiveness of his tone sent spirals of heat swirling through her, temporarily lifting her mood. For the moment, her mind erased all thoughts of pictures, David, or drama. Her only focus was the gorgeous, amber-eyed man on the other side of the phone.

"Yes, this time. I'm going to start working on dreaming up those fantasies immediately. Oh, how you will pay, Mr. Lewis." Her mischievous chuckle filled the air.

"Promises...promises," he whispered in a voice thick with desire.

Dangerous Dilemmas

The next morning, she held the staff meeting she'd been putting off. Clarabelle, Maybelle, Tracey, Carla, Gertrude, Percy and Clarence sat around the meeting table looking at Kayla expectantly. "I need to start off by thanking each and every one of you for hanging in there with me. I appreciate your patience, your guidance and most of all, your loyalty and love. Three years ago, I was a real wreck...didn't know most days if I was coming or going. But you guys were my rock and my strong tower. I haven't totally lost my sanity because of the support I've received." Kayla paused as she'd already said a mouthful before the meeting even started.

Here goes nothing. "Anyway, here we are in a new age, with a different demographic on the island than in years past. I've been thinking that now is the time to try to catch up with the times. We all know that a lot of the machinery doesn't work. Or at least it has a mind of its own and works when it wants to. The grills are temperamental, the fridge is haunted and the list goes on." The small group laughed collectively.

"I'll put my cards on the table. The bottom line is I'm tired. I need a break from the grind."

Maybelle's ample bottom almost fell off her seat. "Chile, you're not talking about selling are you?"

Kayla shook her head decisively, "No ma'am, I'm not going to sell. I'm going to do something better than that. I'm going to turn this place into a state of the art bistro with all the latest equipment and new culinary delights."

Tracey looked down, refusing to meet her gaze. There was a calm silence that circled and enveloped the meeting space. Then, like a category five tornado, all hell broke loose.

"If you think I'm going to get up to cook some damned tofu—"

"Oh, hell no!"

"Miss Kayla, if you do this I'll quit."

And thus began and ended her staff meeting as everyone, including Tracey, walked out. With no staff, she had been forced to close for the day. Kayla put a sign on the door that read, Closed due to loss of power.

There was no raucous talking at the counter. No kids screaming for more pancakes. No teens sitting in the booths laughing and smooching.

But she didn't leave after putting up the sign. Instead, she stayed in the empty restaurant where she sat in the emptiness, feeling like the biggest failure on the planet.

The financial hit she would take for the day couldn't be helped, but she would leave that up to her accountant. Her accountant would fix it…that is, if he didn't quit too, she lamented.

That evening after a long shower, she called Cole. She wanted nothing more than to be held in his strong arms and told everything would be all right. "I miss you, baby," she whispered.

"Not half as much as I miss you."

Cole's reply warmed her in all the right spots as he spoke.

"I've been thinking about you all day, which is probably not the best thing for me as I prepare for my meetings on behalf of the magazine. But enough about me, I think I detect stress in your voice. Are you sure you're okay? Did anything else happen?"

Unfortunately, everything but okay. "I'm handling it," she said after a long sigh. Kayla didn't feel like talking about the Great American Williams Rebellion. She'd had enough of discussing drama for one day. "I need to start the plans for the restaurant renovation—no one else seems to want them except for me. Emotionally, I'm a wreck about the issue. Every time I get comfortable with the notion, something comes up. I've met several times with contractors, and I can't seem to settle on a company. It's maddening, but I'm not giving up. I'll just take it slower than I had originally planned. There's that and…" Kayla sighed again. "We live in one of the most visited tourist cities in the world, but I don't do anything to enjoy myself…well, that's not exactly true since you've been in my life."

"Flattery will get you everywhere; keep it up."

She chuckled. "Has anyone ever told you how crazy you are? I'm being serious. I need a vacation. But I must say you've helped to change

Dangerous Dilemmas

my life. I'm looking forward to new and different experiences—especially in the bedroom."

She smiled into the receiver as the CD player changed to Eric Benet's latest release. She gently swayed on the bed to the melody of his song "Pretty Baby." A few minutes later, she decided she couldn't listen to Cole and Eric at the same time. Two sexy men spelled disaster for her hormones and were just a bit too much for her concentration. She flicked off the CD player while she channel surfed. Two channels later, she was treated to a generous view of a couple engaged in vigorous lovemaking.

With her finger on the remote poised to change it, she hesitated long enough to watch a few moments. *Unh,unh,unh…not what you need to be watching, girl.*

"Are you okay?" Cole asked, as if taking note of her sudden hesitation. "What are you doing?"

Kayla turned the television to mute. "Thinking about how I should hop on a plane to Atlanta. You sure you don't want some company?"

He chuckled. "I'd love it, but only if that company is you."

She was feeling more than just a little naughty. "So, have you ever watched *Shock Video*?" She asked ever so innocently. "I was sitting here minding my own business when it came on. I found some…um…rather interesting positions, which I'd love to try when we see each other again," she teased.

She could hear the smile in his voice as he responded. "Don't talk like that woman. You'll have me on the next plane out of here and back to Hilton Head."

She leaned back in the bed, feeling warm and tingly. The next segment followed an Asian couple who had sex all day. Kayla's mouth fell open when the woman answered the door as her mate pumped her from behind. "Um…I think I'd better change the channel." Her breath escaped in a small gasp.

"What's the matter, too hot for you in the kitchen?" Cole teased.

Kayla chuckled. "Yeah, something like that. And without you here to put out the flame, I'll just end up frustrated and grouchy. You've got me

98

feenin' for you, Mr. Lewis. You're like a drug I've grown addicted to. I may have to find myself a 12-step program."

"Don't you dare. I kinda like it this way. Now, I know I'll get some good lovin' when I see you. In the meantime, you just make sure the television show is the only thing that makes you hot while I'm gone."

She sat up a little. "Not an issue and you know it."

"So you mean I've helped bring out the freak in you, huh?"

"Yes, Mr. Lewis, pat yourself on the back. You got me saying and doing stuff I thought only existed in books." She chuckled again. "Or on HBO television shows."

"Are you still watching the show?"

"No, I turned off the television."

"I'm going to put the phone down. Give me a second."

Intrigued, Kayla wondered what he was up to now.

"Okay, turn to the On Demand channel and select program four on the After Hours menu."

Kayla scrolled through the menu until she found the right show. *Hot Mocha Mamas*. She drew in a sharp intake of air. "Okay, I'm there."

Cole dropped his voice to a low guttural whisper, "Turn off the lights in your room. Then turn the volume to medium. Once you do that, I want you take off all your clothes. Better yet, let's do that together. I'm taking off my socks. Tell me what you're doing."

Kayla darkened the room so only the glow of the television filled the space. Though already naked from coming out of the shower, she decided to play along, adding her own flavor to the game. Before she spoke again, she depressed the speaker button. She had a feeling she would need *both* hands for this little activity. Her low sultry voice purred, "I'm taking off my black fishnet stockings. I'm rolling them down now, slowly. My hands are between my hot thighs as I slide them down further. Now my stockings are around my ankles…now I'm sliding them off my feet."

"I'm unzipping my pants. Damn, I'm growing hard just thinking about you. I want to be between those luscious thighs."

Kayla moaned. "Yes, that's where I want you to be too. My thong is so wet I'm going to have to rip it off. I'm sliding it down my legs, inhaling the scent of my love juice. Hot, flowing and ready for you to lick up."

Cole's raspy voice raked over the edges of her sensitized skin. "Feel my tongue, tasting you…lapping up your wetness. I'm right there with you, baby. I'm taking off my shirt next. Then I'll be naked and ready for you to taste me after I bring you to the brink of sensual madness. I want you to be as crazy for me as I am for you."

Kayla felt the room begin to spin as her breathing became faster. She teased her nipples, caressing her breasts until they tingled.

"Look at the television, baby. Imagine that's us on the screen. Touch yourself for me."

Mesmerized, Kayla watched the couple on the screen engaged in foreplay. Her toes curled after the man began to suck his partner's nipples to stiff peaks. She felt her sex quiver when his mouth moved from the woman's nipples to her clit.

She breathed out slowly, and her fingers kept steady pressure against her sex, bringing her close to the edge. "Feel me, Cole," she said shakily. "Feel my hair, feel my lips quiver from your touch. Feel the fire between my legs, the fire only you can put out."

"Yes," he hissed. "Feel my shaft deep inside you as I pump my head in and out of you. I love your tightness."

"Cole, baby, I'm about to come." Kayla dropped over the wondrous edge of orgasm. Her body shook with her release as she trembled in ecstasy.

"Damn, girl, I love what you do to me."

"Not as much as I love what you do to me," Kayla responded, still breathing heavily.

This was the last day of the trip, and she needed to make her move. Sheila dabbed Red Door behind her ears and down the hollow of her long neck. After one final turn in front of the mirror, she was ready. *It doesn't get any better than this.* Then she left her room, crossed the hall and inserted the new key, smiling to herself all the while. She loved that men were so gullible; it made her work so much easier. Getting the information she needed had been no problem at all.

The dreamy bed felt perfect. The sheets enveloped her as she snuggled deeper. Now, all she had to do was to wait. Sheila stroked herself in anticipation, eliciting soft moans from her plum colored lips.

As soon as Cole opened the door to his hotel suite, he stopped in his tracks. The veins in his neck pulsed in anger. He was livid and his tone showed it. "Sheila, what the hell are you doing here?" He didn't even want to think about how she found him in Atlanta. With her talents, finding out information was easy, but he no longer cared. He just wanted her out.

Sheila sat up on her elbows, the sheet failing to conceal her small, but full breasts. As she breathed out, the sheet fell, exposing her nude body to just above her abdomen.

"Cole, sweetheart, we're still friends aren't we? I was in town visiting friends and thought I'd come by to share some old memories. We had some good times here in the ATL. Do you really mind so much?"

"Sheila, I've told you repeatedly there is no *us*—no matter how many little stunts you pull. What we had was good fun, but it wasn't meant to be forever. Do yourself a favor and move on with your life, as I have." Cole stood by the door ready to open it as soon as she was dressed again.

Sheila's eyes glistened with tears. This wasn't how it was supposed to be—he was supposed to tell her he'd made a mistake and declare his undying love for her.

"Cole, what are you saying? I know we can be good together again. Kayla can never be to you what I am, can never replace me."

"I'm not even going to ask you how you know her name because that doesn't matter. What does matter is that she doesn't need to replace you. She's all I want, Sheila. I'm in love with her. Trust me, you and I are finished."

We'll see about that. With excruciating slowness, she put on the purple Teddy, three-inch stiletto heels and deep purple wet-look trench coat. Sheila blew a kiss as she walked toward the door. "Strike two, lover."

The flat expression in his eyes mirrored his words. "Game over, Sheila." He slammed the door behind her then picked up the hotel phone. "Front desk?"

"What happened?"

"Nothing. Absolutely nothing." Annoyance peppered Sheila's tone. "He thinks the damn sun and moon rise and fall with her. It's pretty pathetic, but I'm out. I'm tired of this. You're on your own. Personally, I don't think you stand any chance of getting her back." Sheila sighed dramatically. "Cole Lewis is sprung. If your Kayla feels the same way about him, the jig is up and we may as well all go a different route." She crossed one long leg over the other. "I'm not usually one to back away from a challenge, but in my humble opinion, this war is over."

David turned to look out the bay window overlooking the city. The sparkling lights and beauty of the Atlanta skyline were lost to him as fury clouded his vision. "Go back again. This isn't over until I say it is."

Sheila stood up, slipped her shoes back on her feet and gathered her purse. Enough was enough. He was starting to creep her out. "I'm tired. I'm going to pour something stiff then go to bed. Call me in the morning."

"Walk out that door without my permission and the first item I'll take away is the car. Next will be your condo."

Sheila stopped in her tracks. The whispered but harsh tone was enough to convince her he meant everything he said. "David, what do you want me to do next? Kidnap him?"

Spinning back toward her, he said, "If that's what it takes, do it. I don't give a damn if you have to ride naked on a horse like Lady Godiva. Your job is to turn Cole's head. I don't care what you do, but I want him out of Kayla's life, and I want it now. *Capisci?* And for the record, I don't lose."

She swallowed hard into a dry throat. *Oh God! He's a maniac.* "Yes, I understand. Whatever you want, David."

"Words to *live* by. Now go on get out of here. I'll call you once I've come up with a new plan, since you seem incapable of doing it yourself."

The biting words struck her like a physical slap. Tears welled in her eyes, but she refused to let them fall. *No wonder Kayla had left him. David Sutton was a sadistic bastard,* she thought.

Self-preservation can make a genius out of the most ordinary person. Sheila headed straight to the lobby of the hotel. If she were going to salvage her life in South Carolina, she would have to do it quickly. She didn't trust anything with David on the loose. It could be months or years before the company addressed his abuse of power. Sheila wasn't taking chances.

"I have a message for Cole Lewis," she informed the desk clerk. Once she handed him the hastily scribbled note she said, "I'll be checking out now. You can leave the charges on David Sutton's credit card, thank you."

The staff returned to work the next day, defiant, but efficient. The customers were served the same great food they were used to and the kitchen mishaps were few and far between. Kayla worked in her office, sipping cola and munching on a chocolate chip cookie that baker extraordinaire Clarabelle had made earlier.

Just as it had taken a little time for her to become comfortable with the thought of change, it would for everyone else too. Once the bistro became a bustling booming business, attitudes would improve.

On the upside, she thought, at least she didn't have a dot matrix printer. The dream bulletin board was becoming quite full. The newest photo was a picture of the new Dell system she planned to purchase. It was going to cost a nice piece of pocket change, but it was worth it in the way she and Tracey would be freed up from archaic paperwork methods. The mere thought of new and modern made her tingly inside.

In the meantime, she would continue to work as she always had. Slow and steady. *One click at a time, but I'll get there.* Smiling to herself, Kayla worked on the agenda to present her new restaurant plans to the staff. Mr. Stone at the bank had been especially helpful in pointing her in the right direction. She had a good list of contractors and a firm budget. The only hitch right now was the time frame and how long exactly the old Williams Diner would be closed. Lost in thoughts, plans and dreams, she worked steadily until one of her young employees interrupted her.

"Ma'am, there's someone to see you up front."

"Thank you, Carla. I'll be up in a second. I just need to finish this last sentence." Kayla gave the girl a crooked grin. "And what did I tell you about calling me, ma'am. I'm old enough to be your big sister—not your mama."

Carla grinned too. "Yes, ma'am, I mean, Miss Kayla."

Kayla hurriedly logged off the computer. She smoothed the creases from her outfit before she walked up to the front. Thankfully, she hadn't seen David in a couple of days. So, she wondered, *customer complaint or compliment?*

"Cole!"

With open arms, he said, "In the flesh. Hope I didn't catch you at a bad time. I wanted to see you as soon as I landed."

Without bothering to wait until they were behind closed doors, she pulled him toward her in a passionate kiss that showed just how much she missed him.

"Hey, hey, take that to the office before the Department of Health shuts us down," Tracey said in jest, coming up behind them.

Finally, good sense prevailed, and Kayla reluctantly broke the steamy kiss. She grabbed his hands to eagerly lead him to her office. "Maybe she's right. Let's continue this in the back."

"My pleasure."

As soon as they were behind closed doors, Cole gave her a tentative kiss…a gentle probing that made her yearn for more.

So, Kayla insisted on more. She knew her employees were right outside the door, but she didn't care...she wanted him. A sly smile curved her lips. As long as she was quiet...

Cole slid his tongue down the length of her neck. She tasted as good as she felt. His hands sought her body. He caressed her arms, reveling in her warmth and softness. He felt himself lengthening with each stroke. Kayla felt him too, and it excited her.

She arched her body toward him. Cole pulled out her shirt, which had been tucked neatly in her pants. The explosion of warmth around her abdomen almost proved his undoing. She felt delicious. He wanted to taste her...

Cole broke away then returned to her mouth and devoured her lips in an all-consuming kiss. His tongue probed deeper. He wanted to taste all of her juices. She tasted like a mixture of mint, chocolate and the Coke she'd drunk earlier. Cole liked it.

Cole continued his sensual foreplay. He knew he would take her right there on her desk. His fingers felt her nipples straining against the silk of her bra. Her sexy lingerie under the conservative skirt excited him even more.

He reached behind to her back and unfastened the bra in one swift motion. Kayla giggled. He was so good at that...

He caressed her breasts, bringing each nipple to life, which elicited soft moans from Kayla. He moved to take her nipple into his mouth. The warmth of his mouth felt heavenly, but it wasn't enough. She needed to feel all of him now!

She unzipped his pants and his hardness sprang up instantly—yearning for her caress. Kayla didn't disappoint. She stroked him up and down until she felt pre-cum at the tip of his penis. She rubbed it around his head before she brought her fingers to her mouth to taste him.

Cole smiled. "You are too much. I don't think I could ever get enough of you."

"Luckily, we won't have to worry about that—I'm all yours."

Cole moved his hips against her body. He wanted her more than anything. He slipped his fingers into her now open pants and felt her moisture. She was ready for him too.

"Lean over the desk for me, baby," he whispered.

"I thought you'd never ask," she purred.

Kayla lowered her pants just far enough for him to enter. She'd worn a thong, which turned him on more.

"What are you trying to do to me?" Cole moved his briefs down over his stiff penis and placed a condom on the throbbing head. He teased her bud with his fingers before he entered her.

She gasped with the first contact. Damn he made her feel good. She gyrated her hips up and down to receive him; she took him in as far as he would go and loved the feeling of his full shaft in her tight space. Their lovemaking was swift, wild and passionate. Kayla bucked against his body, her breasts slapping up against each other while she did.

Cole loved the sound of his body slapping up against her smooth brown ass. He pumped her in and out, hard and fast until he felt himself on the edge. "Baby, I don't know how much longer I can hold out!"

"Don't worry about me," she barely managed to squeak out as her orgasm bubbled to the surface. "I'm trying to wait on you."

Cole held onto her breast and squeezed the tender flesh. He held her tight as he pumped her harder and harder. It was all she needed. Kayla forgot where she was and screamed out his name as the orgasm rocked through her and had her seeing double. She shivered and shook against his body.

This time she made the drive to Cole's place in record time. Despite working all day, her body still hummed from her and Cole's exciting if too brief contact. Tonight, she hoped to pick up where they'd left off.

"I have a little surprise for you. I think we've both been working too hard and need a little *us* time." Cole held up trip brochures and information for their two-night stay in Georgia. "I thought we might be the tourists for once. How does that sound?"

Kayla smiled in delight. "It sounds like heaven. When do we go?"

Cole showed her confirmation of their hotel room. He pointed to the clock on the nightstand. "Hmmm…In about an hour."

Kayla dismissed any objections her more practical side might have had. She was interested in *more* than just a little *us* time as it were. She planned to show him how good it could be between them. *Besides,* she thought, *he still owes me my fantasy.* A naughty smile crept along her lips. "Cole Lewis, you are a man after my own heart. Thank you!"

Savannah, Georgia…

Cole drove the hour from Hilton Head to Savannah. As he neared River Street, he thought about his accident weeks ago but dismissed the eerie feeling of déjà vu it brought. The Hyatt Regency Savannah situated on Riverfront Plaza offered them a gorgeous view of the river street area and all its charm. Their room faced the river and gave them an excellent view of the festivities and activities of the Savannah nightlife.

The beautifully appointed room boasted a large four-poster bed, which was one of the most comfortable Kayla had ever sat on. The room also had a sitting and dining area in the room and exquisite finishing touches. She felt as if she were in a resort in the middle of historic Savannah instead of a hotel room.

Their first activity was a carriage ride through the magical city. Cole had arranged for a Moonlight and Roses Tour, which began in front of the hotel where they were staying.

During the carriage ride, he fed her strawberries and champagne. By the middle of the ride, she was feeling no pain. She snuggled up to him, enjoying his nearness and warmth. A cool breeze came off the river, pushing her closer to him. Cole decided on a simple route for their tour;

they passed through most of Savannah's twenty-one beautiful public squares before circling back to the hotel.

They decided they would walk to some of the museums for a more in-depth look into the city's history.

Upon returning to the hotel, Cole noticed he'd missed two calls from Cassandra. The hotel had come up with the wonderful concept of private booths for people to use their cell phones, thus allowing users privacy and protecting others from the bother of having to hear someone else's conversation. Cole headed to a booth on the end so he could find out what was going on at the magazine. "Let me call the office. I'll be right back."

Still feeling the effects of the champagne, Kayla looked toward the cell phone booth. "I think I'll go with you." Desire lit up her eyes, making the green in them sparkle.

He followed her gaze and smiled. "Hmmm…I like that idea."

Once inside the booth, Kayla lifted her skirt just enough to give him access to her. Cole quickly followed her lead. He unzipped his pants, letting them fall to his knees.

She ripped open the gold foil condom packet with both hands while he gyrated against her.

Cole kissed her neck, tasting her skin as he worked his way down to her nipples. He sucked hard, bringing the bud to stiffness, while he pinched the other nipple between his fingers.

Kayla pushed away long enough to roll the condom up his thick shaft. As soon as she was finished, her lips sought his again for a deep kiss. A kiss that swirled heat from her head to her toes.

She rocked her body against his. He parted her legs with a knee then dipped down long enough to position himself inside her. He stroked gently, but the fire that had built up between them was too strong.

Panting from desire, she said, "Give it to me hard and fast, baby. We'll save gentle for later on tonight. Right now, I need to feel you."

Cole abandoned all attempts at finesse and gave it to her hard and fast, bucking her up against the padded walls of the booth with each strong thrust.

Kayla screamed out his name as her orgasm ripped through every nerve ending. Her body shook with the power of the sensations that coursed through her. She felt Cole's tongue deep in her throat as his body quivered with the power of his climax. It took several minutes for them to recover long enough to actually do what they came to do.

Cole could barely keep a straight face as he spoke with Cassandra. At the moment, work was the last thing on his mind, especially as Kayla skillfully stroked his sensitive sac, which still pulsed from his release. As he became aroused again, he realized that if she kept this up, his call to the office was going to have to be brief…very brief. Kayla Williams required more of his *attention*.

No trip to Savannah would be complete without a visit to the *Lady and Sons Restaurant*. Cole scored major points with Kayla once he showed her tickets to the Paula Deen Tour, which included food, shopping and an exclusive chat time with the star of hometown cooking.

Paula was just as real and lovable in person as she was onscreen. Kayla was almost speechless at seeing one of her idols.

After the cooking tour, still too stuffed to think too much, they set about on their own unguided walking tour where they explored the riverfront area as well as some parts of downtown.

They learned more about Savannah's unique history with buildings dating back to the seventeen hundreds. It is home to several museums, including the *Ralph Mark Gilbert Civil Rights Museum*, which they toured extensively before going back to River Street.

The couple spent a fantastic time exploring the city and spending time together. By the end of their excursion, both felt rejuvenated.

After checking out on Sunday, with some regret, they headed back to Hilton Head.

Cole spoke quietly as he drove. "We didn't make a decision before we left, but I'd really like you to come back with me to my place. I can't imagine waking up and you're not there now. If you let me, I'll be there for you. You'll never have to feel afraid again."

She stroked the side of his face. "You really are too good to me. Yes, I'll let you be my knight in shining armor. I have no desire to handle this on my own any longer."

"Good, then we have a deal."

Her tour of Savannah had given her an idea she thought might work for the magazine. "So, how about adding a food section to the magazine? I've always wanted to share some of my favorite recipes. I've thought about making a cookbook for the restaurant. Daddy always wanted to do one, but I've been so busy I haven't had time. I could probably manage a few short magazine articles."

"I like that idea. Would you be interested in a major catering job? I know you have some personnel issues, but if they can become involved in this project, maybe that will smooth some ruffled feathers. Let me know if you think you can swing it and I'll make the arrangements. In the meantime, feel free to make me your one-man focus group. I think our readers would especially love some easy soul food recipes and holiday desserts."

Kayla's eyes lit up. "When we get back, how about I make us a dessert I've been dying to try out? It's a triple chocolate cake I want to offer at the restaurant for special occasions like birthdays. It is sinfully decadent, but I haven't tested it yet."

"Are you kidding me? Twist my arm harder." Cole grinned. "I'd love to try anything you make." The edges of his eyes crinkled in mischief. "If you have any left over chocolate sauce, we can find other uses for it, I'm sure. I can think of two places in particular I'd love to lick it off." He caressed each nipple to a stiff peak.

Kayla shook her head. "Cole Lewis, you have no shame." She purred, "But I like it."

CHAPTER TEN

Columbia, South Carolina

Always one to know the difference between quantity and quality, Sheila made two mental notes as she looked around his place. David's condominium wasn't as nice as Cole's, but it was adequate, if not sparsely furnished. A feline-like grin crossed her lips. Nonetheless, good location, good address.

David might have been an interesting playmate if he hadn't been so weird and demanding, Sheila thought. He had everything going for him, but he was obviously never satisfied. They were almost two of a kind. But she knew where to draw the line, which is why she had left a message for Cole to be careful after she left the hotel in Atlanta.

Sheila watched David with a keen eye. As soon as she could, she was leaving South Carolina. She was too good for this crap. In the meantime, she would hone her acting skills.

Anger smoldered beneath the surface as David spoke. "I would think with your assets you would have been successful. Maybe you just didn't try hard enough."

A harsh laugh escaped her lips. "Honey, I laid it out there for him every which way but loose, but he wasn't biting. Not anymore anyway. He told me all he wants is her. And trust me, I've tried everything."

David struggled for control. "Is he talking marriage?"

She shrugged, "Who knows, but it sounds like it to me."

"We'll see about that."

His icy tone chilled her. *Yeah,* Sheila thought, *she was definitely out of this particular game.* If this Kayla Williams was so damned important to both Cole and David, they could figure it out themselves. She had other things to do.

Cole was handsome, fit the profile and was a wonderful lay, but there were other fish in the proverbial sea. She didn't need to be hurt repeatedly by him in order to know when she'd lost the fight. True enough, she'd worked a little harder than usual, but that was about to end.

Brought out of her reverie by his next comment, Sheila just nodded her head as she stood up to leave.

David continued, "I'll call when I need you."

At the door, she said, "Until then. I'll keep you posted on what I find out." *Yeah, right, about the time my ass hits the road.*

In the darkness of the evening, David made his way back to Kayla's house. And again, she wasn't at home. He figured if she weren't at the restaurant, then she was probably with Cole, the very thought of which incensed him. The only positive he could take away from this was that it gave him time to do what he needed.

If she had been spending so much time away from home, she probably hadn't had the time to change the locks yet. After he parked, he sat in the car for several minutes to check out the area. He couldn't be sure some nosy neighbor wasn't going to interrupt him. Once the block appeared clear, he jogged from the car to the house.

He fingered the key he'd held onto for the last several months. *Ahh yes.*

His patience had been rewarded as it slid in easily. Kayla was nothing if not consistent.

The layout made it easy to find what he wanted. David walked around the small house as if he owned it. She hadn't changed it much since he'd moved out. The same furniture sat unused in the same spots. She wasn't even like most women, who at least made an attempt to keep things fresh by rearranging the furniture every once in a while.

With a shrug, he headed toward the master bedroom. Their room— well, at least it was before Cole began sticking his nose where it didn't belong. He went straight to her bedroom closet. *So predictable.* All of her important papers were in the same fire safe box, which was nestled among her shoeboxes on the top shelf. He rifled through the papers until he found what he wanted.

In the morning, he would begin to make calls. The thought of how he would begin to pick her life apart was enough to make him aroused. Eventually, she would have no choice but to come to him. He planned to have it all. The business, the house, the car…anything she owned. He planned to own her for her betrayal.

David copied down what he needed then left as quickly as possible. No sense being caught for a simple B & E when he had more important things to do with his time.

4:00 A.M.

Kayla glared at the clock. If it were possible to murder an inanimate object, she would have been responsible for the death of several timepieces. *So, to open or not to open, that is the question.*

Since the meeting where she'd announced the changes, it had been hit and miss. Sometimes she had enough staff, other times they held sick-outs. Kayla sighed. If she could get everyone together, she might have a solution, one they could all agree on. But until she arrived, she wouldn't know. Despite the disastrous nature of the first one, it was time to hold another little meeting.

By the time Tracey arrived, Kayla was working on her second cup of café mocha and knee-deep in paperwork.

"Can we talk?" Tracey asked.

The expression on her face was neutral by design. If Tracey were going to extend an olive branch, she wouldn't bite her hand off. Kayla looked up from her papers. "I would love to. I have some things to talk about as well, but you go first."

In a nervous gesture, Tracey wound her ponytail around her fingers. "I feel like a real criminal for deserting you when you needed me. I still don't agree with what you want to do, but I think I owe you my loyalty, especially as your manager. I can understand if you want to get rid of me."

"I've had some time to take a step back too." She exhaled. "Maybe I was a little insensitive in my approach. I think I forgot the 'family' aspect of this diner. If we can gather everyone now, I'd like to discuss a compromise."

"Everyone is outside waiting to talk with you. I think the plan was we would fall down one by one on our knees and beg your forgiveness. I'm speaking for the entire group. We feel pretty rotten about our behavior and what happened. You've been there for each and every one of us, and we let you down."

I work with a bunch of crazy people. Relief flooded through her tired muscles. "I think it is going to be one of those group hug moments. I need to apologize to you folks as well." Kayla stood up. "Come on, let's go talk."

The group reassembled, and this time, nervous energy was the prevailing emotion.

She started slowly. "Thank y'all for coming back. I think I learned rather quickly that I can't do anything without you guys...you make this place rock." She offered an anxious smile. "I need to know something. If there was a way to keep the diner going, would you stay?"

Miss Maybelle said, "As long as these old hands and this body hold up, I'll be here."

Kayla looked around the nodding heads. She smiled inwardly. She didn't tell them near enough, but she loved her crew. Young and old. "Then I have a new plan."

Pulling out her writing tablet, she began with her first point.

"Okay, I don't know about anyone else, but 4:00 A.M. is kicking my natural behind. I'd like to open two hours later on weekdays and three hours on weekends. There are plenty of fast food places to take up our slack. Besides, after the construction crew clears out, our regulars don't come in until later."

"Thank you, Jesus," she heard from the belle sisters.

A smile curved her lips. *Amen.* "As a family diner, we don't need to be open seven days a week. Our operation is too small and you guys need more time with your families. We've all been burning the midnight oil, giving our blood sweat and tears to the restaurant, but I don't think we need to continue to operate this way. I want my crew to stay." A warm genuine smile spread across her face, a smile that was returned by her staff. "During the holidays and summers, we can extend the hours, but during the fall and when the majority of the tourists are out of town, we can reduce our hours." She cleared her throat. "Also, I want to cut back by a day. We can still maintain a good profit if we aren't taxing the machines, equipment and, of course, you guys so much. We already shut down the restaurant for one week for vacation. Why not a little more in order to continue to keep up the quality. We do well. Our food is fresh, delicious and, most of all, made with a generous portion of love. You can't beat that, and most of all you can't replicate what we do in another location. This diner is an icon in the area. I realize now how important that is to the community." Kayla put her tablet down to look each person in the eye. She could tell they were in agreement and that the tension in the room had abated.

"My plan is to make it easier on ourselves while we serve the community we all love so much. Change is not always easy, but soon enough they won't even remember the way we used to do business. Okay, now these last two points are the biggies."

She clasped her fingers together to stop them from shaking. "I'm going to update the equipment so we can have a more efficient and safer kitchen, but any other changes to this establishment will be cosmetic. My promise to you is that I'll listen to your suggestions. Let's keep the doors of communication open."

And for the big finish. "I'm going to liquidate some of my own personal assets to open my dream restaurant. I've decided that Hilton Head is big enough for two Williams establishments. I'm going to start looking at property that's close to here. I have to follow my dreams. Y'all know that I have a love affair with food. I love the down-home dishes that we make, the food that comforts people and keeps 'em coming back for more. But I can't wait to create new and exciting dishes. Clarabelle, I just might make something with tofu…but don't count on it."

Clarence asked, "Well then, what will you call it?"

"I haven't decided yet. I'm thinking *KW's Bar and Grille*. Another reason I wanted to talk with you guys as a group is that I'll be in Chicago for three days. The trade show is coming up, and I'm hoping to get some new ideas for the diner as well as the bistro." The heaviness of tension and stress started to dissipate more. Kayla felt a reconnection to her staff. The confidence she felt in her decision grew. *This is going to work*, she thought and thanked heaven above.

"The bistro is several months to a year in the making, so my first priority is and will continue to be the diner. I'm asking Tracey to stay as manager, but I'm also looking to fill an assistant manager position. Before I leave, I want to know if we're in agreement." Kayla leaned back in her seat. "So, what do y'all say?"

After a great morning, things began to go downhill. Busy with her new plans, Kayla put the phone on speaker while she worked. The energy drain of drama quickly replaced her good mood.

"Ms. Williams, this is Mid-Atlantic insurance. Our records show that the payment you sent in for the Williams Family Diner account was returned for insufficient funds. We need to make other payment arrangements in order to keep the account current."

"Ms. Williams, I'm calling about your car payment. The audit of the loan indicates your loan had some back charges. Accordingly, the loan has not met the terms for payment in full as previously indicated. We need a payment to cover the back charges as soon as possible."

"Ms. Williams, I'm afraid we've run into a problem with the loan. We're going to need to look at your tax returns and profit and loss statements for the last five years."

Take three. Kayla put her head in her hands when the phone rang again. "Let me guess," she responded to Mr. Stone, "You received an anonymous tip?"

"Well, I can't really go into detail."

Score another point for David Sutton. "You don't have to. I know who is making my life a living hell. Just give me a couple of days to put the information together. I'll fax it as soon as possible."

"Detective Duncan, major crimes."

"Hi my name is Kayla Williams. I was transferred to you to talk about my situation."

"Yes, ma'am, how can I help you?"

She exhaled. "I think someone is trying to hurt me…well, not just someone, my ex-boyfriend, David Sutton. I think I need a protective order or something. I'm sorry. I'm so nervous, I don't know what I'm saying."

"You're doing fine, but I need to know specifics. Has he ever physically hurt you? If so, have you filed a police report before?"

"Well, no. He's never been violent before, and I've never filed a report against him. There have been several mishaps at home and work. I think he's trying to sabotage my life. He comes to my restaurant, and then I see him outside my condo at odd hours almost every day."

Dammit, she thought, the story was starting to sound crazy even to her own ears.

"I understand your concern, but unless we have more, there's nothing we can really do. I can have extra patrols in your neighborhood though…sometimes that's enough of a deterrent. The same thing goes for the restaurant. We can have an officer come in regularly. I know it doesn't sound like much, but other than trespassing, we aren't going to have much of a case."

That much she knew. "Okay, well thank you. I'll keep you informed."

Disappointed didn't even begin to adequately describe her feelings. David was going to win…again.

"What time do you think you'll be leaving the office tonight?"

"I've got some material to go over with Robert, but we should be able to wrap it up in a couple of hours. Are you okay?"

"I will be. I'll see you soon." Kayla sat back in her chair, wondering what was next. She didn't want to have a pity party, but she didn't know how to combat David's attacks either. The only reason he let her go before is that she lost her usefulness. But now, he wanted her again. For some ungodly reason, he wanted her again, like she was some damned carnival prize.

Kayla wasn't foolish enough to think love had anything to do with the way he felt. Everything David ever did in his life was about power and control. He wanted it all.

By the time Kayla made it to Cole's place, she had made up in her mind that no matter what it took, David wouldn't run all over her. She discussed the disruptions in her life with quiet determination.

They sat on his bed while they talked. With a calmness and surety that she didn't feel, she said, "He's attacked all of my accounts. My credit cards, checking and savings, car, mortgage and insurance. He's a sneaky bastard, and because he's in banking and information technology, he can pretty well do anything he sets his mind to, so I'm screwed until he undoes it."

Unable to believe his ears, Cole tried to come up with some way to help her. "No, you're not. In the morning, cancel whatever you can live without. Fax proof of your record keeping for the other things and notify the credit reporting agencies of fraudulent use of your accounts. Kayla, you're not alone. Whatever I can do for you, I will."

She'd never had to be bailed out financially as an adult. Kayla seethed inside as she thought. If David actually screwed up her A-1 credit rating, there would be no helping him.

Heat turned the tips of her fair-skinned ears red. But pride and good sense didn't go together. She had to be practical if she were going to maintain her life.

Kayla looked down almost too embarrassed to speak. "I really hate to ask you to do this for me, but until my accounts are straightened out, I'm going to need to borrow some money."

"Just name it, it's yours. We won't let David get away with this Kayla, I promise. The police may not be able to do anything for you just yet, but I can. Perhaps a call to the bank where he works—we need to fight fire with fire."

A wan smile crossed Kayla's lips. "I don't have proof; that's my problem. If I could prove what he's done, I could stop him. Right now, I have to fix each area one by one."

"What he's doing is fraud. Maybe you can't prove it's him right now, but there's no denying someone is messing with your accounts. Your first call needs to be to your bank. And correction, *we* have to fix each area. Kayla, you are not going to go through all by yourself. If I need to leverage my business or sell something to help you get the restaurant off the ground, I'll do it. We'll also find a way to prove whether he's behind this. Sweetheart, I know it's easier said than done, but try not to worry. You still have the sale of the house to depend on for cash reserves. Your loan for the restaurant doesn't depend on it. David is cunning, but there's only so much he can do."

"Yes, I know, but how deep will this go? I'm hoping the house won't be complicated as well. I have a meeting with a realtor in a few days." She paused, expelling a long, tired breath. "I need to go by the house to make sure everything is in order. Maybe I should have someone house sit for me. The thought of David being in there without my permission makes me feel...violated. I know it probably sounds silly, but I do because he invaded my space. I've been in that house for five years. It was my first major purchase, and even though we lived in it together for a few months, he had no right to invade my privacy like that. Maybe one of the first things I should have done is put a lockbox on the door."

Cole wrapped his arms around her as he spoke. "Sounds like a good idea. In the meantime, I want to help you get settled in over here as soon as possible. You can put your things in the second bedroom for now." He chuckled. "For the first time in my life, this doesn't seem like enough room. Guess we'll be house shopping sooner than we thought."

The heat from his body provided a welcome respite from her dark thoughts. Kayla turned her focus to Cole and how good he made her feel. Tomorrow was soon enough to deal with all the drama. For right now, she had more important things to turn her attention toward.

"So you're ready to have me here full time, huh? You're just saying that because you think you're going to have greater access to my body. Don't think just because I'm going to be here you can jump my bones daily."

Feigning shock, he said, "Oh you wound me with your low assessment of my character. I plan to jump *dem* bones at least twice daily."

Kayla chuckled. "Okay, that's better." She settled into the bed then said, "Hmmm...my first order of business is to paint all the walls bright pink."

The sound of Cole's laughter warmed her heart. Despite the seriousness of her circumstances, she felt quite content snuggled up against Cole. *Damn you, David, for trying to mess this up.*

The next morning, Kayla explained everything to Tracey, swearing her friend to secrecy until a solution had been worked out. After she took care of the credit cards and Mr. Stone's requests, she felt a little better. But with more thought, Kayla came up with another plan to address the mess David had created.

"Kayla, I understand you think you need to do this, but I'd feel better if Cole knew and were going with you."

A small sigh escaped her lips. "I know, but I don't want things to get out of hand. David is manipulative, not violent. At least with me there won't be a physical battle. I have to do something. I can't just keep waiting to see what's next. Besides, I don't know how far he'll go. I have to try to stop him now."

Perspiration dotted along Kayla's hairline as she spoke to the receptionist. "Mr. Sutton, please."

The attractive African- American girl seemed somewhat suspicious of her, for reasons Kayla had no idea.

"Is he expecting you?"

Uh...just do your frickin' job. She didn't have time for this. "Just tell him Kayla Williams is here to see him."

"Yes, ma'am, I'm sorry. I should have recognized you from the photo on the desk." The woman brightened visibly. "I'll tell him and he'll be right with you. Before you go in, though, I'd just like to add my congratulations on your wedding engagement. The honeymoon sounds divine too."

The overwhelming desire to faint attacked her for only the second time in her life. Kayla nearly hit the floor. Kayla watched as the receptionist's finger reached within half an inch of the button.

"I'm sorry, I feel terrible, don't tell him I was here." Without waiting for a response, she dashed out of the building.

Kayla gulped air as if she had been drowning. Gawd, she was so stupid. Why did she continue to be surprised by the things he did and said? David was never going to change…and he certainly wasn't going to listen to reason.

"And you're sure it was Kayla?"

"Yes, sir, she left her name. All of a sudden, she said she wasn't feeling well though. She rushed off before I could even offer her water or something else. She did look pale."

"Thank you, Janice. I think I'll go home to check on her. I'll just finish the rest of the day working out of my home office. Call me on the cell if anything important comes up."

Well, this is a good sign. So what can I do for you, Kayla? Come to beg me back, beg for my forgiveness? David felt the familiar tug in his pants whenever he thought of being with Kayla again. He imagined her warm lips kissing his, making him feel like a true man. He'd always loved the feel of her tight body writhing under his as she called out his name in passion. Or better yet, he would hit it from behind; he wanted to hold her small hips with his large hands and pull her toward him hard and fast just like he used to do. His bulge grew in anticipation. She needed to be at home because he didn't feel like running all over town looking for her. She'd made the first step; now he would do the rest. A small groan emanated from his lips. He stroked himself, ready to make up for lost time.

We'll just see…If you play your cards right, I won't make you beg too much.

Kayla sat in the car for almost an hour just thinking. She didn't want to tell Cole what she'd heard; it would just make matters worse. But how was she going to deal with David? *Wedding…honeymoon…*David was losing touch with reality.

Would Detective Duncan be more inclined to do something now? David was starting to believe his misguided fantasies. Surely, the police would see that now.

"I don't know how he can get away with this! There should be some way to show that he is using his knowledge and know-how to hurt someone. Kayla doesn't think the police will do anything because he hasn't harmed her and we don't have proof he's making calls to disrupt her life, but I'm not going to sit around and let him destroy her life. She's going to be moving in with me officially soon enough, but I still don't feel like she's safe. I damned sure don't want her going back to her house without me or someone else with her."

Robert ran his hand over his head in frustration. "I feel ya, man; this ain't gonna work. How's Kayla holding up?"

Shaking his head, Cole responded, "She's hanging in there, but with everything that's going on at the restaurant too, I think she's emotionally drained. She doesn't deserve this. I'm trying not to make things worse for by going after the guy and ripping his head off...she doesn't really want me involved in this at all. I don't see how I can stay out of it any longer, frankly."

"So, what's going on there? Any long term plans? Are my pallbearer services going to be required any time soon? I'm off David right now— I'm just plain being nosy."

Cole smiled for the first time during their conversation. "Like I don't know the difference? And that's best man, which I may have to fire you from. But to answer your question, I'm ready, but Kayla on the other hand... Ahh man, what can I say? We take two steps forward and three back. I know she loves me, but she won't admit it just yet. She's the most stubborn woman that I know."

"Well, what's she waiting on? Her moving in is a good step though. If she's willing to do that, take advantage of it. My best advice is just to go home and give her that Lewis loving. If she needs to work this out on her own, don't crowd her. I know as a man you want to fix it, but maybe she's the only one who can. Sounds like David is trying to force communication between the two of them. If so, maybe he'll chill out once he realizes how happy she is with you. Or maybe he'll go psychotic and you'll have to kill him. If that's the case, I'll help hide the body."

"Will you get out of my office? Some of us have real work to do."

"I'm going, but maybe you should check into what sort of review boards are available for banking officials? See if the burden of proof is on you or on him. If he's responsible for Kayla's mishaps, maybe he's not as smart as he thinks. Could be he messed up and left some sort of trail that can lead back to him."

Cole looked up at his friend, his interest piqued. "I knew there was a reason I kept you around. I'll start calling now. Kayla will start to breathe a little easier once she gets some control back in her life. She's so used to being in control and independent. This is killing her inside."

"Well, what happened? Did you see him?"

"No, but I talked with his receptionist. Apparently, he's going around telling everyone that we're to be married. He even has tickets to Hawaii for our honeymoon." Kayla closed her eyes to block out the pain.

"Oh my gawd. You haven't even seen this fool in months. He's gone totally delusional, Kayla; you need to be careful. I'm not trying to end up on Lifetime."

In spite of the seriousness of what she said, Kayla grinned and shook her head. "All right for the queen of drama. So, now what? The police have been no help, and I'm afraid Cole will go off the deep end if it becomes physical between them. He's ready to jack him up, which is out of the question. I can't survive off the occasional conjugal visit, so I don't want him to take things into his own hands. Besides, with David so out of control, he might actually try to hurt Cole. I don't know what I'd do if something happened to him." Kayla paused while she put her head on her chin.

Tracey leaned in closer, asking in a quiet voice, "Have you told him how you feel about him yet?"

"Why do you want to complicate things for me? I'm struggling hard enough to control my emotions. In case you haven't noticed, I've been a bit of a wreck lately. I don't see how telling Cole I'm madly in love with him and want to have all his children is going to make much of a difference. I have been the biggest punk lately. I'm trying to go forward not backwards at this point."

Tracey grunted. "Damon and I may not be talking marriage, but he knows I love his dirty drawers. Call me crazy, but I think if you stop fighting the way you feel so hard, you might be pleasantly surprised with the results."

"Yeah, and what kind of results would they be?"

"Laugh at me if you will. But I'm happy I don't have to wear the pants, and when I need something, I ask freely. Control ain't all it's cracked up to be. Nobody is saying throw away all your shoes and start having babies. For me it's about knowing that as much as I give, I'll get it back. Sometimes, I get a heck of a lot more."

"I think I need a good stiff drink."

"I think you need a good *stiff* piece of Cole. Now go home and tell him everything so you two can figure out what to do next."

"Damn, with advice like that, how could I go wrong?"

Smirking, Tracey said, "I do what I can. Now scoot. I'll see you back here after your trip. Have a good time in Chicago. Try not to eat too much on the Navy Pier and souvenirs for staff are welcome."

"I'll see what I can do about that. Thanks for the talk." She glanced at her watch. "Hmmm… I need to run by my house to pick up a few things, and then I'm going to Cole's if you need me."

David watched as Kayla pulled her red Saab into her driveway and raised the garage door. "Good girl, you didn't disappoint this time." He stroked his still hard bulge. Smiling, he opened his car door to approach her.

CHAPTER ELEVEN

Sweaty palms were something David had never had to deal with before. Why did Kayla make him nervous? He smiled inwardly. The answer, he knew, was because he'd spent so much time away. She'd grown into a stronger woman. She was still the beautiful, intelligent woman of his dreams, but it seemed she was a bit more on the feisty side with her parents' death. The old Kayla wouldn't have resisted him like this. Damn, he'd almost forgotten the flowers. He turned back to the car.

As he reached in to pick up the bouquet, he heard the sound of another vehicle approach. He turned to recognize it as the blue BMW that Cole drove. David swore vehemently. Cold fury seemed to push ice water through his veins. Cole Lewis had become more than a little problem. If Kayla were coming to see him, then Cole was now interfering with whatever she sought to do. His breathing came in ragged drags as he struggled for control. Anger caused him to crush the stems of the flowers he held absently in his hands. Blood from the rose thorns trickled from each puncture, but he didn't care. Soon, he would see Cole's blood leak from his body. He had half a mind to take care of him on the spot.

Instead, he watched. *Patience, you're almost there.*

Kayla looked up surprised. "Hey, what are you doing here?"

"Just came to see what I could do to help. I talked with Tracey earlier, and she told me that you might be headed over here. To be honest, I didn't like the thought of you being here by yourself, so here I am."

"Well, come on in. Since I haven't been here in awhile, I don't know what it looks like." She paused in thought. "I'm going to have to get rid of this house soon. I hate for it to be here empty."

They walked in together, after Kayla perused the yard. She needed to find a neighborhood boy to cut her grass and tend to her flowers. It wasn't too bad yet due to the cooler weather, but she didn't want the house to look vacant. Not good for the curb appeal, she thought.

Once inside, Kayla began to open the windows to air out the house. "Will you get the two bedrooms for me?"

"I don't think I ever took note of how nice this property is. This is a great location too. I think you'll probably be able to get the top price for it."

Next, she assessed the kitchen. It was time to start boxing up dishware and figuring out what to give away and what to keep.

She leaned against the sink.

This was the first place that she and Cole had been intimate, but it wasn't enough to erase the memory of the time she'd shared here with David.

"What's that look for?" he asked.

"I don't know, maybe just a touch of melancholy," Kayla replied as she tucked her hair behind her ears. "This house was such a major purchase for me. I was only twenty-five and spent over one hundred thousand dollars on it. I thought I would about stroke out during closing, yet here I am, ready to dump it as fast as I can. Funny how quickly plans and priorities change."

With outstretched arms, he came to her and guided her into his arms. "Is that what you want? I don't want you to feel pressured about moving."

A gentle smile curved her lips. "No, I don't feel pressured. It's a woman thing. I'm okay, really. Change is good. I'm moving on to fresh and different, and I'm happy about that. Besides, I think we both need to start over in a new space to make new memories, ones that are just ours, if you know what I mean?" *No David and no Sheila.*

"Can we add this to the list of experiences?" Cole covered her mouth with his warm lips in a possessive kiss.

"Ummm...I think that can be arranged."

Several minutes and several kisses later, Kayla packed up a few items to take with her. As she walked out of the house, she knew it wouldn't be for the last time yet, but her attachment would never be the same.

She had to look toward the future now, no sense looking back. Like Miss Maybelle said, she had her own destiny. The house represented where she came from, not where she was going. Kayla gave the lock one final turn and she was finished.

Now, she thought as she watched Cole get into his BMW, *onto bigger and better.*

Planting kisses along her jaw and neck, Cole asked, "Are you sure you don't want me to go with you?"

"Um...your lips can go, but you have to stay here," Kayla teased.

He nipped her earlobe in response.

"Hey, watch that." Kayla moved away from his wonderfully tortuous mouth and swatted him playfully on the shoulder.

In a fake wounded tone, he said, "I knew it, all you want is my body."

"Yeah...so, what's your point?" Kayla said with a giggle. "It's not just that body I love either; it's the delightful way that you use it too. Now, before you make me late for my flight, will you hand me my bags?"

The four-hour flight from Hilton Head, S.C., to Chicago was made much easier by pleasant thoughts of Cole. Kayla leaned back in her chair with a slight smile on her face. Cole had insisted on paying for everything for the trip—including first class flight accommodations. *I could get used to this...*

The only way it could be better was if Cole were beside her, she mused. A small sigh escaped her smiling lips. But she couldn't complain too much. After all, they did have a *very nice* farewell. Kayla touched her lips, which still tingled from his kiss.

Irresistible, sexy, and wonderful... It would only be for three days, but she would miss him. It still amazed her how much she'd fallen for him in so short a time. Her feelings in her ill-fated relationship with David had never been like this in all the time they were together.

Her nipples responded to her thoughts as they pressed against the fabric of her bra...tight and stiff. But Kayla resisted the urge to soothe them with her hands.

The desire to be with Cole was always there. It didn't matter if it was three days or three hours away from him, the feeling would be the same. He'd become as much a part of her life as breathing.

The bottom line, she'd realized, was that Cole Lewis had taken over her heart...and she didn't mind a bit. By the time she landed in Chicago for the restaurant event, she was ready to call him just to hear his voice again. *Just focus girl,* she laughed at herself. *You'll make it. And once you do, maybe you can show him exactly how much he was missed with a few tricks and a few purchases from an adult toy store.* She was grinning in devilment by the time she disembarked from the plane.

The National Restaurant Association's annual event was the must-attend event of the year for anyone in the food, hotel or motel industry. On her first day on the floor, just as in times past, she felt like she had stepped into a fairytale.

The exhibits, the new gadgets, the presenters, and workshops...added up to a wonderful experience. She read the program as if it offered up the answers to the meaning of life. She spent a wonderful day at the convention then went back to her room, exhausted, sated and blissfully happy. *Damn, this is almost as good as being with Cole.*

There was only one way to end such a good day. After a relaxing shower filled with good thoughts of her lover, she settled down between the heavenly sheets of the bed. It was so temptingly soft, she didn't know if she would make it on time to the morning workshops.

But she knew sleep would not come until after she heard Cole's velvety smooth voice.

"So tell me how much you miss me; tell me how you don't know if you can take another breath without me by your side. Or you could just tell me about your day." She purred into the phone.

"And you call me crazy. But yes, I have found it to be a disappointing thought that you will not be in the bed next to me tonight. I love having you intertwine those long legs of yours around mine. I love that loud snore that threatens to knock the shingles off the roof."

"Oh you! Just wait until I get back." She chuckled along with him. "So, no mocha mamas tonight?"

"Only if you're up to it. I've been running around all day, but I'm game if you are."

Kayla thought about it, she was too tired for fun and games tonight, but it warmed her heart that he would go along just to please her. *Damn, you're lucky girl.* "Rain check until tomorrow night? I think I'd rather just listen to you whisper sweet nothings in my ear until I fall asleep."

"The way you use me is just shameless. Do you feel any remorse?"

"Nope, not a bit," she said, barely able to keep the laughter out of her voice. "You know I'm just joshing you. But on a more serious note, I do miss you. I've enjoyed waking up to you as well, even though it has been at a most ungodly hour. I like where we are, Cole. I hope you do as well." She felt a certain nervousness at her sudden candor. *Girl, what are you doing?* "I'm sorry, maybe I shouldn't have said that."

The prolonged silence between them increased her anxiety. "Cole?"

"I'm here, sweetheart. I'm just processing. We've joked around about our feelings so often, I feel I need to be clear. I care about you, Kayla. Since you've come into my life, I feel more settled emotionally. You've made me feel more complete, something I didn't think I'd ever have, not with the job and my schedule. I'm in a different space emotionally, and I have you to thank for that."

"I haven't done anything, Cole. I'm nobody special."

"Yes, you are. You're special to me. And once you return, I'll show you just how much."

"Now those are the words I want to hear. You've got two more days to take your vitamins."

Stifling a yawn, she said, "With that said, I think I'll say goodnight. My long day is starting to catch up with me." *You're making this complicated, Cole Lewis!*

"Okay, dream about me."

"Always."

The next day Kayla spent time going to the exhibits and demonstrations where she would learn the most about creating the bistro of her dreams. She loved the comfort food she served in the diner, but a workshop on nutrition trends was particularly interesting to her.

There was no way to stop Miss Gertrude from trying to put the whole pig in with the collard greens. Besides, there would probably be another revolt if she tried to stop her, but at least she could start with a clean slate for the new restaurant.

The International Cuisine Pavilion also caught her eye. Her plans for the bistro included serving menu items with European flair. Hilton Head catered to the southern palate very well, but as the type of traveler to the area diversified, Kayla felt the menu options should as well. She smiled as she envisioned sleek surfaces with a modern edge. Her plan was to serve food that tasted great and was good for you. A small giggle escaped her lips.

For as long as she could remember, butter was a part of her life. Her mother, Anke, had subscribed to the philosophy that more butter was better. As a tribute to her, however, she planned to serve Danish pastries from her mother's authentic recipes in the morning. She had goose bumps just thinking about what it would be like.

The last stop of the day was the kitchen innovations area. It was a gadget lover's paradise. Every new fangled way to do something was on display there. Ice cream in forty-five seconds—no problem.

At the end of the day, she went back to her hotel room feeling exhilarated. She'd collected a bag full of goodies to take back to South Carolina…ideas and innovations, but most of all dreams. She celebrated with a bubble bath and a little champagne.

As she nibbled on her chicken wrap and sipped her mimosa, she thought, *David could give it his best shot, but there was no way he would destroy this for her.*

Filled with positive feelings and buoyed by her determination, she called Cole. This time she had the energy for a little Mocha Mamas and anything else he had in mind.

The return from the show was just as exciting as the flight going to it, but for entirely different reasons. She'd missed Cole, and she wanted nothing more than to relax in the comfort of his arms.

The baggage claim area was abuzz with the activity of travelers and family members or friends, but the only person Cole saw was Kayla. The three days they had been apart seemed like much longer. "You are a sight for sore eyes."

A delighted smile brightened her entire face. "Not half as much as you. Next time, we travel together. I really missed those lips."

"Which ones? These?" His soft, full lips gently brushed against hers, and then, in an insistent kiss, he devoured her mouth. Tasting her, teasing her, bringing out the fullness of her passion.

The blaring of the turnstile buzzer broke the kiss. Cole grinned. "Guess we should get your bags, huh?"

The words escaped as a small sigh, "I suppose so, but only if you promise to kiss me like that again."

"Count on it."

While they waited for her bags, Cole caught her up on the latest news. Ten minutes into the conversation, Kayla couldn't focus any longer.

As he opened the car door, Kayla sighed then said, "Chocolate, champagne, caviar on soda crackers, fresh pineapple chunks, strawberries, bubble bath and rose petals on 800 thread count Egyptian cotton sheets."

Cole smiled. "Is this a list I should be writing down?"

"Nope, it's just what's on my mind. We can do the debriefing later, but right now, I want to be with my lover doing my best to fulfill old fantasies while making new ones. I have a few surprises in my luggage. Ones I hope you'll like."

Cole gathered her closer to him. "I like the way you think, Ms. Williams…debriefing officially over. If you don't mind a stop on the way home, I'll see about checking off some of those items on your favorites list."

"Promises, promises, but I do like the way you think too, Mr. Lewis."

Once they arrived at his house, Kayla was treated to a nice surprise. Cole had prepared a nice meal to welcome her home. They dined on shrimp in coriander and lime sauce atop a bed of steamed rice along with steamed green beans on the side. "Just a little bistro fare to get you in a French mood."

She put her chin in her hands. "And just what sorts of French things did you have in mind to do, *Monsieur* Lewis?"

"Well, since *Le Français est la langue de l'amour*, I suggest we begin with lots of French kisses."

"*Oui, oui, mon amour*, I couldn't agree more." Shivers of delight followed each tender touch from his warm mouth. For dessert, he had prepared a simple dish of a single scoop of vanilla ice cream topped with a sauce prepared from warm bananas, Amaretto, and banana liqueur. He fed her the warm fruit with each kiss.

Ummm, ça c'est bon.

Much later in the evening, they shared kitchen-cleaning duties then, after a warm shower, settled down to prepare for bed. Naked atop his king-sized bed, Cole treated Kayla to a special "Lewis" style spa treatment. He began at her toes. Cole licked each one, paying homage to each big toe. Up and down, he licked, savoring their shape and feel.

Then he moved upwards, kissing her sensitized skin all the way to her inner thighs. Kayla gasped in delicious agony.

Cole placed chocolate-flavored oil on the tender skin under her breasts, continuing his sweet torture there—he was lost in her softness and the glorious way she felt beneath him.

His lips explored every visible inch of her beige skin. He trailed hot kisses from her neck to her abdomen, causing sweet pulsations in her core. Then he licked her nipples to firm, light brown peaks, causing her to arch her naked body toward him for more.

They made love until the wee hours of the morning, proving to each other just how much each was missed.

The next evening Kayla played catch-up from her trip to Chicago. With brochures, models and measurements in hand, she walked around with the pictures of the new equipment she planned to order. She would be saying good-bye to the two temperamental grills, the inadequate and old refrigerator, and the scratched and dented stainless steel sink in her first order.

Excitement rippled through and charged the air. "This is it," she whispered. After she grabbed her clipboard, she drew out the new layout on a piece of graph paper, closed her eyes and let her imagination do the rest. After several seconds of silence, a single tear rolled down her cheek.

This was the right thing to do, but it felt like such betrayal. There was a certain amount of comfort in turning on the same grills that her mom and dad had turned on for all those years. Getting rid of the machinery that was a part of their family history was like saying good-bye all over again. It had been painful enough three years ago.

She wiped away the tear before she went back to her clipboard of notes. Several minutes later. Kayla had gathered herself enough to make it through the rest of the evening.

"Evening, chile. What you still doing here?"

Startled, Kayla stepped back, her heart galloping wildly in her chest. She wasn't used to anyone staying late, she could usually depend on the solitude of the night.

"Miss Maybelle, that's a question that I should ask you."

A slight chuckle rippled through the quiet space between them. As usual, Maybelle's skin was scented with lavender and lemon. It must have been an old recipe, because Kayla remembered it even as a small child. "Sometimes when I don't feel like hearing Clarabelle and Clarence carrying on, I'll come back and make something for the next day. I was contemplating making biscuit dough. It keeps well enough for the next day's baking." The older woman hesitated before she spoke again. "And you, darlin', what's going on in that head of yours?"

"Well, first off, I had no idea that Clarabelle and Clarence were keeping company. How did I miss that one? And second, well, I'm just dreaming."

A full out smile crossed Maybelle's face at Kayla's comments. "You always did have that sassy tongue. Times, Anke would come back by the refrigerator hopping mad at you, but James would always get after her. Oh whee, was you a daddy's girl, his pride and joy."

"I'm sorry, Miss Maybelle, sorry that I upset you before. You've always been so good to me and to the family. Mama and Daddy depended on you like I depend on Tracey."

"Yeah, that red-haired tart is good for some things. She does care about this place, and she genuinely cares about you. Just keep her arms length from that nice Cole you've been keeping company with—if you know what I mean."

This time it was Kayla's turn to chuckle. "Yes, ma'am. Tell me what it was like in the early days. The days when this old stove was new and all the rage."

Maybelle held her gaze. "I could, but I won't. It's time for you to stop going backward now gal. Tradition is good, but I've been thinking on it. There was a reason you weren't born in 1940. You're of a different era. Time you did things like a young, college-educated gal did them. We did a lot the old-fashioned way cause that's all we had, but not anymore.

They got convection ovens that can cook a twenty-pound turkey in twenty minutes. Times have changed…guess there's no law says we can't too."

"Oh, Miss Maybelle, it means the world to me to hear you say that. I just wouldn't want Mama and Daddy to be mad at me. I don't want to dishonor what they started."

"Ah hush now. If Anke is mad, trust me, James has your back. Just keep these doors open and giving folks the best food they're going to have all day. Your parents are up there watching you, proud of you as I am. Take heart; your new plan is a good one."

Kayla smiled. "Thank you for saying that about my parents. Guess I'll never stop missing them or needing them. But, the diner will continue to be a success, especially with you making pies and biscuits. We can't lose." She put down her clipboard to hug Miss Maybelle. "Now go home and get some rest. We'll both be back here soon enough."

The talk with Maybelle was enough to boost her confidence and buoy her spirits. With work finished, she turned her attention to the rest of the night. Cole would arrive any minute now to take her back to his place. Knowing him, she wondered what delights he had in mind for her—he wasn't a man to half step. He was a man who knew how to *keep company* very well.

She licked her lips. No, Cole definitely did things with a bang. And what a delightful bang it was…

Kayla felt the now familiar throbbing sensation at her core. The folds of her sex begged for his special kind of attention. She resisted the urge to pleasure herself while she waited for him. Damn he made her hot!

"Ms. Williams, we're done. There's a man waiting for you outside too."

Kayla nearly jumped out of her skin. She was so enraptured of her thoughts of Cole, she couldn't concentrate on anything else. She locked the safe and gathered her keys.

"Thank you, Simon. I'll…I'll be right there. Great job tonight. I'll see you tomorrow."

The teenager's goofy smile warmed her heart.

"Thanks, Ms. Kayla. I'll see you after school."

Kayla felt the flush begin behind her ears as she walked out of her office. Cole was ooh so good for everything except the concentration. She just hoped Simon hadn't noticed the effects of her erotic daydreams.

Expecting to see Cole out front, Kayla happily closed and locked the door to the restaurant. It wasn't until she smelled the cigarette smoke wafting through the air that she realized her mistake. The crew had left, which meant she was alone in the dark parking lot with David.

She walked herself through several deep breathing exercises before she approached him.

"You're waiting for me?"

The look in his eyes bordered on lewd. "Yes, beautiful. I came by to see how you were doing. I've been working late, so I haven't been able to come during regular hours."

"David, what makes you think we are friends? I've been patient with you, but I have zero desire to see you again. You made me miserable while we were together. Why would I want to go back to that when I have someone in my life who loves me?"

Anger flashed across his face. "Kayla, I did things I'm not proud of, but I'm not the same man as I was before. I'm sorry you feel that way about us, about what we had, but I caution you against thinking Cole Lewis is perfect." He reached out to stroke her face, but Kayla moved out of his reach.

"Don't. Just don't. I want you to leave me alone. Don't ever come here again. This is my property. If I have to, I'll get a restraining order against you."

Cole drove up. David took one look at him, then moved away to get into his car. Before he did he said, "Ask Cole about the woman he was with in his Atlanta hotel room." With a wink, he said, "As for the restraining order, you already tried that, remember. Good night, sweet Kayla."

"Kayla, are you okay?" Cole asked. He watched David drive away at break neck speed. "Sweetheart, what did he say to you? You're trembling."

Fear tightened around her heart like a vise grip. She couldn't go through this again. If Cole had been unfaithful after she gave him her heart, she would never forgive him.

This can't be happening. Kayla blurted out, "Cole, how could you lie to me? How could you take my feelings and walk on them like this? I trusted you and you twisted my feelings into nothing with your betrayal." Tears fell from her eyes, but she didn't care. Nothing else mattered right now.

David replayed the vision of what happened over in his head. The expression of hurt and pain in Kayla's eyes made him uncomfortable. He didn't enjoy having to hurt her in order for her to listen to reason, but he decided that, if necessary, he would do it again. *And she didn't even put up a fight. She just believed the worst of Mr. Wonderful.* A victory smile split across his face.

He dialed Sheila's number. As soon as she answered, he quickly told her what he wanted then hung up.

After he closed the phone, he felt a lot better. Things were looking up…Now, to put the next part of the plan in motion. David felt better than he had in a long time.

Cole felt like he was a part of a bad movie. This should not be happening. *Damn you, David Sutton.* He should have known Sheila would do anything to sabotage his relationship with Kayla. "Darlin', it's not what you think. Let me explain everything, but not here. Let's go home."

Humiliation and hurt were mirrored in her eyes as she spoke. "We don't have a home. Take me to my house, please."

"Kayla, just listen to me."

As his request was met with her stony silence, Cole decided to leave well enough alone. She needed time to cool down. He blew out an exasperated breath, but he knew she would calm down...eventually. David obviously knew which buttons to push, so now she would have to figure out how to deal with that. Cole trusted that, as soon as she thought everything through, she would be ready to talk. And he would be ready to explain his ex-girlfriend's ridiculous behavior. David and Sheila had just officially plucked his last nerve.

Ms. Sheila Pickwell, yeah, it was time he had another little talk with her. The fact that she hooked up with David was more than a bit disconcerting. She was a spoiled diva, but he never imagined her hanging out with someone so malicious.

Cole turned on his Eric Benet CD and drove. The short distance from the restaurant to Kayla's place seemed to take an eternity in the black silence that surrounded them.

Once there, Kayla mumbled thank you and hurried up the driveway into her house. She shut the door quickly behind her before she could run back to Cole to beg him to take her with him. She didn't want to be in her house, especially with David lurking around.

Kayla listened to the rain pelting against the window. Several minutes later, it was followed by thunder and lightening. *Perfect.* Just what she needed, a thunderstorm. As a little girl, she hated storms with a passion, and as an adult, she hated them because her parents' crash occurred during a storm.

Kayla fought hard to keep the tears at bay. A battle she quickly lost as a trail of hot tears fell down her cheeks. She succumbed to a feeling of misery so intense it was physical pain.

CHAPTER TWELVE

S heila, what the hell have you done?" Cole leaned back in his leather chair. His intention to work at home had been destroyed by the inability to concentrate. After a while, he'd given up, grabbed a Smirnoff, and dialed Sheila's number.

"Whoa, you don't call me, kick me out of your life, and then talk to me this way? I don't think so. You've got three seconds to change your tone, or you can listen to the sound of me clicking off this damn phone."

"I don't have time for your games. Tell me why you would hook up with Kayla's ex-boyfriend?" He took a long sip of the drink before he continued. "Why are you trying to destroy my happiness?"

She breathed heavily into the phone. "Don't be so dramatic, but for your information, I left a message for you to tell you to watch out for him at the front desk of the hotel. I don't think either one of us knows what he's capable of doing."

"I didn't receive a message before I checked out of the hotel. Nonetheless, it doesn't excuse what you've done or your behavior. I want it to stop and I want it to stop now."

"Don't try to bully me, Cole. I'm not even in Hilton Head any longer. I've relocated to North Carolina with my sister…so lose this number because I'm certainly going to lose yours." With a heavy sigh, she added, "David doesn't even know that I'm gone. I'm not proud of being so damned desperate, but you don't have to worry about me. I got it now. Look, I apologize for some of the things I've done, but you're a big boy. I'm sure you can handle it."

The slight tremble in her voice indicated she wasn't quite as strong as she portrayed. "As for me, just as you've suggested, I'm moving on with my life. Good-bye, Cole."

"Not so fast, Sheila. I want you to tell me what you've done. I don't want anymore surprises."

"I haven't *done* anything. But I am done with this conversation. Have a happy life with your precious Kayla. Take care of yourself. Just watch your back. David Sutton is the type who won't take no for an answer. He doesn't exactly subscribe to the three-strike rule. I don't think he's going to stop until he has no other choice."

Unfortunately, given what he'd seen of David's behavior so far, he was inclined to agree with Sheila. Cole finished the Smirnoff and tossed the bottle in his trashcan.

You should have taken out the trash long ago. Now, as for David, his three strikes were up—he would see Mr. Sutton in the morning.

Kayla had tried her way to no avail. Obviously, some people need a bigger hint before they moved on. Sheila had finally come to her senses, now it was David's turn. *Yes, it was definitely time for David to go*, he thought.

The next morning after a completely miserable night, Kayla sat at her kitchen table trying to figure what had happened. If Cole was trying to humiliate her, he was doing a damned good job of it. Kayla took another tissue out of the box and dabbed at her nose…mad that she was even crying again. This bordered on being ridiculous.

You have to get yourself together. Of late, she and Tracey hadn't been quite as close, but right now, she needed her friend. *Somebody needed to be honest with her*, she thought miserably. She trusted Tracey with her no holds barred attitude, so she called her. When Tracy said, "I'll be there in an hour," Kayla had never been happier to hear those words.

As soon as Tracey arrived, they went to Kayla's kitchen to sit down.

The hair pulled into a ponytail, pink bathrobe and slippers stopped her in her tracks. "Honey, I'm not trying to be mean, but you look like crap. What's going on?"

Kayla smirked. "Well, as long as you're not being mean, say what's on your mind." After she balled up the tissue in her hand, she said, "I'm so upset with myself. I can't stand this. I don't want to be a weak woman who lets a man walk all over her. But I feel like such a fool. I don't know what to think anymore."

"Well, it sounds to me like you are quite 'sprung' and you're fighting it."

"No, I'm not. I'm dealing with my feelings for Cole. I'm just afraid of being duped. I mean what if he's fooling around. Think of the irony. David, my ex, tells me that Cole cheated." Kayla shook her head in disgust. "I feel like a friggin' candidate for Springer."

"How many times do I have to talk you off the ledge girl? I'm telling you, find out from Cole what happened and don't give in to David Sutton's games. The man is a master manipulator. You've said so yourself, so why give him the satisfaction of ruining your new relationship? Find out at least if there was a woman, and if so, damn, make sure it wasn't his cousin. You didn't let the man explain, did you?"

"What if he cheated?"

"What if he cheated? Kayla, listen to yourself. There is no dilemma. Not unless you continue to let David have his way with you. Find out first then worry about what to do. If you love him, decide if you want to keep him. But if you don't, leave the buzzard alone."

"You do have a way with words." Kayla tucked her hair behind her ears. "I'm sorry to whine like this. I just feel so discombobulated."

"Hang in there, hon. Things will start to slow down, and if they don't, then maybe they will begin to make better sense. Sometimes you just have to white knuckle it until you get through. Sleep on it and call him in the morning."

Two days without Cole. "Maybe you're right. I do need to talk with him because imagining all the wrong things he may have done is driving me crazy. I feel like David is still calling the shots, and that makes me even more upset. Why do I let that ass push my buttons?"

"Now that's something only you can control. As long as he gets off by making you jump to his tune, he'll do it. David Sutton is just a man. He may play like he's omnipotent, but he's got to eat, sleep, and crap just like the rest of us. The sooner he figures that one out, the better off he'll be too." Tracey wiped her brow dramatically. "Now, where's the pie?"

Later that evening, Kayla had hyped herself up with coffee and sweets; now she was trying to come down off her caffeine and sugar enough to go to sleep. She lay in her bed feeling exhausted, disappointed, hurt, guilty and humiliated.

In truth, she wanted nothing better than to call Cole, but she couldn't just yet. Tracey's words had struck a cord. What was honestly in her heart? Did she love him like she should? She couldn't take him through changes like a teenager enjoying her first crush. She needed him to know that he could count on her and vice versa.

Kayla swallowed hard into a desert dry throat. With so much going on internally, she found it difficult to focus on any one issue. It was almost a case of déjà vu. Some of the same issues that had affected her relationship with David now affected her relationship with Cole.

Kayla decided that, if she had been hasty in her assessment of the situation, she would be eating quite a bit of crow in the morning. In the meantime, she just had to hope that Cole wasn't so disappointed in her that he wouldn't accept her call. *You made a real mess of this one, didn't cha?* A long, tortured sigh escaped her lips. Despite 4:00 A.M. coming very soon, it was going to be another long dismal night.

12:30 P.M.

It was time to make the rounds of the diner again. Kayla felt the need to get back to her normal routine. So much had changed in just the last three months. Maybe that's why she felt so out of sorts.

She smoothed down her black skirt, tucked her stubborn hair behind her ear then left her office. Change was good, but sometimes, continuity was better.

The diner was alive with activity. Kayla waved to regulars and newcomers alike. The longer she moved around the restaurant, the better she felt.

Inhale...exhale...breathe. Her heart felt as if it would pump out of her chest, despite her willing it to stay in. Cole sat in a corner spot off to himself. *I guess no one felt the need to tell me he was here!* Hmph, she would deal with them later.

She gave him a tentative smile. "Hi."

The smile he returned to her was warm and loving. "Hi, yourself. Do you have a minute to sit down?"

"A minute, then I need to get back. I planned to call you later, if that's okay?" Her heart continued its assault against her ribs, beating wildly and erratically. Kayla sat down while she awaited his answer.

"It will have to be very late. Robert and I have a conference with some agents." He paused, and when he spoke again, his voice was low and restrained. "Kayla, I did not betray your trust. It sounds lame as hell, even to my own ears, but I swear to you, I did not invite her. Sheila was in my bed naked once I returned to my room from a meeting. I asked her to leave immediately, which she did more or less. It wasn't exactly pleasant between us, but she did leave. Baby, I love you," he added softly.

The tension oozed from her body. She didn't want to believe what she'd heard from David, but it was easier to go with the worst. Hurt and shame reflected in her green eyes as she lifted them to look directly into his. "I am such a fool. Will you forgive me?"

"No."

"No?" His teasing tone intrigued her.

He casually lifted his drink to his lips. "Not until you fulfill my wildest sexual fantasy."

"Oh my, Mr. Lewis, you do know how to put a girl on the spot. How much time do I have to decide on this deal?"

As Cole leaned toward her, she felt the heat of his desire. Cole brushed her lips with a kiss so light it sent shivers of anticipation racing through her.

Unable to adequately control herself around him, Kayla stood up before she closed the distance between them and kissed him like she wanted.

A lascivious grin curved his mouth. "I'll expect your penance to be completed tonight."

As she walked away, she said softly, "You do drive a *hard* bargain. I'll have to see if I can satisfy your terms."

His mischievous smile sparkled in his amber brown eyes, which nearly proved to be Kayla's undoing. She supposed it wouldn't be right to kick everyone out so she could make love to Cole on the spot.

"Wicked woman…That's what I'm counting on."

Kayla went back to work, thinking about just how she and Cole would make up. Tracey walked in as Kayla remembered her bodice-ripper fantasy.

"Oh my, I'd say by that look your conversation with Cole went well."

"You might say." Kayla responded coyly. "Thanks again for the pep talk. Sometimes I don't know what I'd do without you."

"Just remember me at bonus time," Tracey joked. "But seriously, I'm glad you talked; now, quit giving the man so much grief. He's obviously crazy about you, and you wouldn't act so emotional if you weren't crazy about him. Enjoy that fine specimen of male magnificence."

Kayla chuckled. "Trust me, I've learned my lesson. And for the record, I plan to enjoy every inch of him tonight."

In dramatic flair, Tracey held her hand to her forehead. "Oh my ears. I'm too young for all this…just give me the written report tomorrow. By the way, I meant to tell you how proud I am of you. You hung in there, girl. What that scumbag tried to do wasn't kosher, but you didn't give in, and that's what's important."

"Thank you. I stopped the bleeding for now. Mr. Stone understood and luckily, because I only had a few credit cards, it worked to my advantage to either close accounts or just get new numbers. It's working out…I'm not out of the woods yet, but I'm certainly more confident about all this working in my favor. Cole has helped tremendously too. Now, out of my office, woman," she said as she pointed to the door. Smiling broadly, she thought, *a written report, that girl is too much!*

Even tired, she was the most gorgeous woman he'd ever known. Cole had had great timing. As soon as he'd pulled up, Kayla and the crew were ready to lock up the store. He turned the CD player to the same Gerald Albright selection she had enjoyed at the club and waited for her to join him in the vehicle.

"You are a sight for sore eyes. I've been thinking about you all day."

Kayla smiled. "The same goes for me. I just hope you didn't make me forget to do something important. You have wreaked havoc on my concentration since I last saw you—so what are you going to do to make up for it?"

Amused, Cole said, "Hmmm, I thought I was the one to have my fantasy fulfilled? Nonetheless, I may have a few surprises in store for you, you never know. I would love to spend time making things up to you. I'd love to spend lots of time with you—period."

Kayla's breath caught in her throat. "You're very important to me, Cole. You've awakened in me feelings I thought had died when my relationship with David ended." She reached out to touch the side of Cole's face. It was meant to be a tender sentiment, but it served to stoke Cole's desire as easily as if she'd kissed him passionately.

Cole leaned toward her to pull her into his embrace. It was not his intention that they make out like hormonal teens in the car, but he needed to feel her close to him.

Kayla accepted all he had to offer. She didn't care that they were in his car outside her business…she just wanted him.

Cole muddled her thoughts and turned her body into a blazing inferno. Her tongue delved deep into his mouth and tasted his sweetness as she explored him.

His kiss matched her intensity…her sensuality. She felt Cole's hands move along the front of her uniform blouse. He caressed her in circular motions, heightening her pleasure. Her breasts rejoiced in the feel of his hands against them…her nipples immediately stiffened, stimulated beyond her control.

Kayla moaned as Cole pinched the sensitive flesh of his nipples between his fingers. She desired him…throbbed for him…needed him…

A moment alone with him and she was creaming. He did very sinful things to her libido. "Cole, I think you'd better drive or we'll never make it home. I'll come back for my car later."

He gave her another toe-curling kiss. "You're right, let's get out of here."

Kayla pulled away from him and readjusted her clothing in her seat.

The drive back to his house was quick, thanks to the lateness of the hour. But time apart did nothing to diminish their eagerness for each other. They practically raced from the car to pick up where they'd left off.

Once inside, Kayla decided to make a little game of it. She unbuttoned her pants with excruciating slowness. She felt herself wanting to be touched. She ran her hands up and down her thighs, and then unzipped her pants. The bulge in Cole's pants began to grow, but she still didn't give him permission to touch her yet.

With her thumbs, she pushed the fabric of her pants away and let them ease down her quivering thighs. Standing in a pool of her own clothing, she purred, "It seems one of us is overdressed…what should we do about that?"

In two steps, Cole reached her and swept her up in an all-consuming kiss. Pent up passion was spent as he took her all in.

Kayla gasped for air. The world disappeared, and the only sound she heard was her heart beating in perfect time with his.

Cole finally broke the kiss and stepped back. "See what you do to me? I have no will power around you."

Kayla smiled. "Yeah, and I like it."

"Come on you little vixen. Let me get your bath."

Her body felt cold as soon as he moved away, but he was right. The sooner she started, the sooner she could have him again. She chose lavender from the scents he had available, and soon the entire bathroom with the delightful whirlpool bath was wrapped in the aroma

Kayla finished undressing and submerged her body in the heavenly swirl of bubbles and fragrance.

Cole had disappeared, but when he reappeared in the bathroom, he held a tray filled with caviar, hand-wrapped sushi, chocolate candy, black grapes and sparkling wine.

"I hope you know I could get very used to this treatment." Kayla's voice sounded like a sultry whisper. She took a sip of the wine.

Cole leaned in close, careful to avoid the bubbles and the water. "Don't you know that's the whole idea? I want you to be so comfortable you never want to leave me."

Kayla gave a little splash, and the bubbles ended up on his face. "Well, you could always join me."

Cole held her gaze as desire welled in his golden brown eyes. "I thought you'd never ask."

He stripped in front of her with the same deliberate care she had taken.

Kayla marveled at the rippled muscles of his abdomen and chest. For a writer, he had the best body she'd seen in a long time. Cut arms, shapely thighs and the cutest golden brown butt. *Yeah, your mama done good.* Kayla blithely enjoyed his game of striptease until he reached for the band on his briefs...then her breath caught in her throat as she watched his arousal become more apparent. He was beautiful and he was all hers. Kayla felt like a very lucky woman.

Naked in all his golden glory, he entered the tub with her. She scooted up so he could sit behind her. The warm water grazed the tips of her breasts, causing her already revved up hormones to surge more. Cole had a way of keeping her in overload. She had only one cycle when it came to him—Hot!

She wanted him more than she thought possible...she loved him more than she thought she could ever love anyone.

Cole turned up the pressure setting on the whirlpool, which surrounded them both in a whirl of bubbles. One of the jets pulsated water near Kayla's most sensitive spot. Combined with the slow circles Cole made around her nipples, she was on fire. Kayla moaned in pleasure while he teased her with his tongue and fingers. She could feel how her reaction energized him—his arousal fit snugly against her back.

Cole moved from her nipples, which now jutted out in their excitement to the warm space between her legs. He gently slipped his large fingers inside her, pulsating her clitoris and bringing her to the edge of orgasm. Kayla panted, her breathing became rhythmically timed with his fingers—he pushed in and she inhaled...he withdrew and she exhaled.

"Stand up for me, baby." Cole's demand was gentle but insistent.

Kayla stood with her back to him. He laved kisses up her thighs and across her buttocks. Slowly, he turned her to him. In the process, he kissed every square inch that was in his path...her sides, her stomach and her navel.

He pushed her legs apart so that he could finish with his mouth what he'd started with his fingers. With gentle licks, he brought her heated moisture to a pool. Satisfied, he continued to play with her while she experienced new heights of pleasure. He held her firmly as his tongue delved deep into her inner folds. He sucked her sex, bringing the nub to life. Kayla was shaking now.

Cole squeezed her cheeks as her body began to buck and convulse with her orgasm. Kayla grabbed his hair to pull him closer. Cole gave it all to her, he licked and sucked her until she was no longer in control and screamed out his name. She stood open for him, crying, while he drank in every available drop of her juice. Tears of ecstasy flowed from her eyes while the moisture of her passion flowed freely down her legs.

It took several minutes for Kayla to recover. When she did, she looked down at Cole and shook her head. "You need to come with a warning!" Several Dutch expressions came to mind, but she would share those with him later.

Cole smiled. "And what would this warning say?" he asked playfully, satisfied with his ability to please her.

"It should say: Man capable of bringing woman to tears; be entered at your own risk."

Cole let out a bass-filled laugh. "Hmmm, guess I'll have to take that under advisement."

Kayla noticed his erection was just as hard now as before he brought her to orgasm. *Let's see what I can do about that.*

Kayla turned around again with her back to him and lowered her body back into the water. Cole moved back to make room for her, but she motioned for him to stay put. She grabbed a condom from the ledge of the tub then made good use of it. Still slick and hot, she positioned herself over his erect member and slid him inside. Cole was surprised, but went along—happily.

Kayla enveloped his long, thick shaft in her hot, wet space and braced her arms on the side of the tub. She moved up and down on his penis in alternating strokes. She took him all in, and then she took only the tip in quick strokes.

Cole knew he wouldn't last long with this sweet torture. He encircled her body with his arms, to bring her closer to him, making her take even more of him. Kayla felt his hands on her breasts. He caressed her nipples to stiff peaks, and they both boarded the ride to ecstasy. Cole's breathing became labored. He was gulping air as he moved closer to a hot orgasm.

"Damn, woman, you're trying to kill me."

Kayla felt the pressure of his touch on her nipples grow stronger. She pumped as hard and fast as she could from her position. She was too close to hold out much longer. "Come on baby, come on Cole, come for me, baby," she encouraged. He squeezed her nipples hard and Kayla exploded. Cole growled out her name seconds later in a mind-blowing climax of his own.

They floated in the stratosphere of their lovemaking for several more minutes. Finally, they emerged from the tub, exhausted but exhilarated.

"Come outside with me. I want to watch the stars on your deck."

He looked down at his bathrobe. "Shall we go *au naturel*, or do I get to put some real clothes on?"

"Hmmm…well, the robe is really working for me and such easy access, but if we don't get dressed, I don't think we'll see many stars."

"I beg to differ. When I'm with you, I always see stars. Constellations, the moon, the sun…"

She wrapped her arms around him. "My incorrigible poet. One kiss, then we can go outside for some fresh air."

"Deal, but there's no time limit on that kiss right?"

Fifteen minutes later, they stood on his deck, each with a glass of *Asti Spumanti* in hand, watching the stars as the wind rustled through the air.

Fall was around the corner, cooling down the South Carolina nights. The temperature had dipped, but their passion for each other remained as heated as a low country boil.

Kayla leaned against his chest while his arms circled around her waist. "Where are we headed, Cole Lewis?"

"I hope toward forever. I don't want to be without you because my life hasn't been the same since I met you. Whatever you want, my love, it's yours—exclusivity, monogamy, living together, or more. I want to give you everything you desire."

Kayla shook with emotion. She'd been kidding herself. She'd never be able to walk away from him—from the love and security he offered. He meant the world to her, and despite her effort to keep the relationship from becoming too deep, she was all in, as they say in poker.

She turned to him. "Cole, I want it all too. No one else has ever made me feel this way. I love you and I want forever too."

He exhaled long and deep. "Do you know how long I've waited to hear that from you? I can't imagine waking up another day without you next to me. We can live anywhere, my place, your place, just as long as it's *our* place."

Kayla paused. "I know that you mentioned not wanting kids right away, but maybe we should move into a four bedroom unit just in case." Kayla took a nervous breath. "That way we will have an office and an extra bedroom."

Cole couldn't hide the excitement in his voice. "Don't play with me, woman. I'll have you moved out before you come home."

Kayla laughed. "I know I squashed the idea before, but I'm starting to like the thought of being with you every night, not just some nights. But before you call the truck, we have some things to work out, so just slow down there. We need to come up with a budget and plan for it. I want a nice sized place so we can have room to spread out. I love your condo, but if I were here twenty-four seven, we might start to get on each other's nerves."

"Speak for yourself. I'm looking forward to when I don't have to wonder if I'm going to see you at night."

The gentle kiss she placed on his lips signaled her agreement.

The excuses for leaving work in the morning or middle of the day were becoming harder to come up with, but David figured he only needed a couple more days to put his plan in full effect.

After Cole left for the day, David slipped into his house unnoticed. He took off his jacket and walked around. He had watched and waited from a spot down the road from Cole's unit.

He had to hand it to him—Cole had a nice place. It was small, but it held all the amenities quite nicely. He had a living room/dining room combination that he'd decorated mainly in black. He used white and red accessories to give it a clean, crisp feel.

David grunted. He didn't want to be, but he was impressed. He went to the kitchen. It was an entertainer's kitchen. Smooth, black granite countertops, double sinks, and plenty of appliances and gadgets occupied the space. David gave a wry smile. Yeah, if he had something this nice, he could throw down, he thought.

Off the kitchen, he noticed a small family room. Cole had two leather sofas and a large screen television, which David was drawn to—he pushed the power button on the remote, and the entire system lit up. "Sweet."

David then turned to a music video channel. *Nice...*Beyoncé was shaking her ass on 52 inches of High Definition resolution. *Very nice.*

The second bedroom also had a full bath. It too was handsomely decorated in a dark masculine color palette.

The office was off the main hallway just as Sheila had indicated. He went to the door, intent on finding out all the pertinent financial information he could on Cole's financial portfolio. If he played his cards right, he would have Cole in bankruptcy in no time. He could tie up his finances for years. Now that was a delicious thought.

David tried the door, but it was locked. *Damn!* He didn't want to break it. He didn't want to give Cole the opportunity to make any arrangements. Kayla had come out of her situation pretty well. But he wasn't quite through with her yet. She would build her new restaurant when he was ready. In the meantime, she could watch lover boy squirm.

Okay, plan B. I'll just have to find some other way to get the information I need. Or better yet, have Sheila find it.

She hadn't been as useful as he'd originally thought she might be, but she wasn't a total loss either. David took out his cell phone to call her. The recording said her number had been disconnected. *Damn you, Sheila.*

Delayed, but not deterred. He took one last look around Cole's place before leaving. With a derisive chuckle he thought, *Enjoy it while you still can. Life as you know it is about to change.*

Dangerous Dilemmas

David left as quietly as he'd entered. Tucking the key in his pocket for safekeeping. He planned to return again. Very soon. And once he did, the real fun would begin.

CHAPTER THIRTEEN

My two little neighbor boys came over again for dessert. Remember them, the two that nearly made me wet myself while they hid in the bushes?"

"Oh yeah, the little boogers who escaped the babysitter," Tracey said.

Kayla continued to pack as she talked. "Yes, good memory. Those two are something else. And can they eat! Anyway, they have me thinking. I hate to be one of those women who claim not to want kids," Kayla said. "But then, after they move in, change their minds. It's just the longer I'm with him, the more I love the thought of having a little Cole underfoot."

"Oh brother, don't tell me the bio clock is ticking? If it is, hit snooze and keep going."

"And here we have it folks, words of wisdom, by Tracey." Kayla snickered. "As I was saying before I was so rudely interrupted, I don't think that the clock is ticking necessarily, but I guess I just want to feel that our lives are perfectly content. I'll be twenty-nine in a couple of months, so I have a little time, but for the first time in my life, I'm actually thinking about it. I mean, with our genes, would our child have green or brown eyes, brown or black hair, it's kind of cool to wonder, you know."

"Uh...no." Tracey laughed. "I guess so, but personally, I know Damon and I aren't ready, so I don't think about it at all. I'm way too selfish. The last thing I want to think about is driving a minivan and running for PTA president."

That comment stopped Kayla in her tracks. "You know, it's a good thing that you're my friend because you are crazy, and I don't know if I could hang out with you otherwise. I can see you on *Desperate Housewives*, probably running Wisteria Lane."

Without missing a beat as she taped the last box, Tracey responded, "Damn right. I'd have those ladies straight."

Hours later, Kayla and Tracey were still chuckling over silly things as they loaded up Cole's BMW X5 3.0i for the last time. It had been an all day process, but as per their deal, Robert and Cole were going to unload and unpack, then at the end of the day, Cassandra and Damon joined them to round out the party.

Once everything was put away, the six of them sat in the living room exhausted but satisfied. Kayla's transition over to Cole's place hadn't been so bad after all.

Kayla and Tracey worked in the kitchen, finishing the preparations for the low-country boil meal, while Cassandra took care of the table.

The men, Cole, Robert and Damon, on the other hand, uncorked and popped the top off anything they could put their hands on while they talked trash.

The three of them were situated strategically in front of the big screen television. As they watched the Spike channel, their testosterone-filled conversation ranged from sports to business to how to keep a woman satisfied. Kayla expected them to pull out and *measure* any second.

The party lasted until the early hours of the morning. Fortunately, with a boil the clean up was minimal. A trash bag, some napkins, and newspaper and it was all done. Leaving the rest of the night for more *intimate* activities.

Cole lay naked next to Kayla in their bed. "Welcome home, Ms. Williams. How was your first night as an official resident?"

Kayla sighed. "Ummm…very nice. But I think I'm missing something."

"Oh? What might that be?" he asked.

"I think we need to toast."

Cole's broad smile lit up his face. "You mind reader. Have I told you lately how much I love you?"

"Yes, but I think I need to hear it again."

They toasted each other by taking a sip of the drink, and then she set the leaded crystal glasses down again.

Kayla dipped her finger in her glass then put her finger in her mouth where she sucked erotically.

Cole reacted instantly, which was just what she was looking for.

Kayla lowered her already sultry voice as she asked coyly, "Hmmm...how should we celebrate?"

"I think I'm supposed to be giving you my confessions of love, *n'est ce pas?*"

She giggled. "I love it when you talk dirty to me."

He captured her lips in a deeply passionate kiss. When he came up for air, he said, "Wait until you see what else I have in store for you." Cole rolled her onto her stomach.

He set her body aflame. The slight stubble from his chin grazed her heated skin, spiraling sensation throughout her body.

Kayla moaned in excitement. Anticipating the next rush of sensations, she arched her body toward his lips. Her breathing came in short pants. She was on the verge of losing control from his ministrations. The first ripples of orgasm caused her body to shake. The delightful combination of Cole's tongue and fingers pushed her past the point of self-control. Kayla's long mane of brown hair shook from side to side as she let go to enjoy a mind-blowing climax.

The next several weeks were devoted to the renovation of the diner and the process for buying the new restaurant, which meant Kayla, had to sell her home. With the magazine celebration also coming up, time was of the essence, since she was also helping with that project as well.

While Kayla leaned up against her doorframe reviewing the realtor's notes, Bobby and Jojo's mother, Melissa, came over to her.

"Hi, Melissa," she said cordially. "How are those pie eating boys?" They shared a laugh.

"Hi there, they are just fine. Growing like weeds as most boys do. So you guys are moving huh? I spoke with your husband, David, just the other day. The boys have talked with him, but I hadn't seen him, I guess because of my crazy work schedule. Anyway, what a nice man you have, you're lucky to have found someone so devoted."

The color drained from Kayla's face, leaving an ashen hue.

For the rest of the afternoon, she waged an internal battle about whether to mention David's snooping around her house to Cole.

In the end, she decided there was no sense in making a bad situation worse. Despite David's best efforts, she and Cole had been able to weather the storm of everything he'd thrown at them thus far. They would just have to continue to deal with him until they had enough to go to law enforcement. David's visits to the diner had tapered off. He had not been a constant nuisance for which she was glad, but knowing he could be lurking around any corner was enough to unnerve her. And she understood that to be part of his manipulation. Besides, her time at work and with Cole prevented her from having to deal with his antics too much.

The anniversary celebration started tonight with an awards banquet. Kayla decided she wouldn't worry Cole with more David drama right now. After having to deal with all her problems, he needed to focus on the details of the celebration. This was Cole's time to shine; he'd been preparing for this moment for the better part of five years.

Let's just hope you're making the right decision. She wouldn't mention David, Sheila or drama. Tonight was about the party sponsored by the one of the local radio stations. Cole had lined up an excellent list of entertainers, from jazz to rap to rhythm and blues. The radio station planned to play the top hits from each year Cole and Robert had been in business. Several months of coordination had come down to this. It promised to be a star-studded event with awards and music…an A-list, invitation-only shindig.

An event she still needed to get ready for. She had thirty minutes to make it on time to get her hair done. After her hair, she had to dash to pick up her gown from the fitter. This was her man's event, and she planned to represent him, she thought smiling. With no more time for worry, she gathered her purse to head out the door. As much as she was looking forward to the party, it was the Williams-Lewis after party that really had her excited. *Freixenet, here we come.*

"Wow!" Cole stroked the side of her face. "You take my breath away."

Kayla grinned at his reaction to her. She'd worked hard to ensure he only had eyes for her. The strapless, iridescent, taffeta gown she'd taken great pains to find gave her a classically beautiful appearance. The hand beaded bodice accented her firm breasts to just the right height—sexy without being overdone.

"You don't look so bad yourself. Is that an Armani tuxedo?" She winked as she goosed him.

Cole turned around as if on the runway. "You like?"

"Very, very much." Kayla waggled her eyebrows. "I'll be sure to carry a stick under my dress to beat the women off you."

"Not a problem. The only woman I'll ever care about is you." As if to prove it to her, he pulled her into a passionate embrace. His lips sought hers, softly, intimately, and then more impatiently. They had a little time to make up for, to his way of thinking, and he wanted to start right now.

"Cole, don't start what we don't have time to finish."

"Oh, I intend to finish all right. We've got about twenty minutes before the limousine arrives; that's plenty of time." He paused for dramatic effect. "Hmmm, now where was I?"

His warm mouth on the hollow of her neck sent shivers of delight through her. Finally, she responded, "You are such a nut. How did I get so lucky?"

The slow, drugging kiss was his response.

As publisher of the magazine, Cole was invited to plenty of after-parties once the awards dinner was over, but the only place he wanted to be was in Kayla's arms. There were plenty of functions throughout the week for him or the two of them to attend, but there was only one here and now.

He planned to take Kayla back home to show her just how much he preferred her over the glitz and glamour. Cole took her in his arms as soon as they cleared the door. He'd been tempted to make love to her in the limousine but decided he could wait. Barely.

He slid her zipper down, letting the gown in all its finery fall to the floor. Kayla stepped out of the flow of the fabric wearing nothing but silk thigh high hose attached with a garter belt and a thong. Cole growled in appreciation.

She twirled for him. "I take it you like?"

"Very much so." He said as he began to undress. Kayla winked. "Let's take this to the bedroom. I want to go slowly tonight."

"Music to my ears, even as badly as I want you."

Cole took off his jacket, loosened his tie and began to take off his shirt, when Kayla stopped him. She pressed her body against his as she slowly unbuttoned each one. By the time she finished, Cole felt his heart about to pump out of his chest.

When her hand slid down to his growing bulge, he knew he was in trouble. "What was that about going slow?"

A giggle was her only response. As she caressed his thick penis, she unbuttoned and unzipped his pants. Then she slid her hands around to stroke the rounded shapes of his firm ass.

His designer pants and silk boxers ended up in a heap as well. Cole wrapped his arms around her, closing the space between them. He felt a little part of heaven as his lips met hers. He deepened the kiss with each stroke and dip of his tongue. There was no time to get under the covers as they tumbled atop the comforter, giving in to heated desire.

Kayla could feel his hard penis as it pulsed and throbbed, waiting on the opportunity to meet the softness between her thighs.

Cole moved from her lips to her exposed breasts. The light brown nipples waited to be tasted, to be teased to hard buds from his willing tongue. *Umm…* He felt her hands move from his buttocks to his hair. She pulled him closer to take more of her. He gently nipped her with his teeth. "Is this what you want, baby?" He sucked harder and she moaned louder.

"Yes, yes, suck me baby." Hearing her say it increased his desire for her. His body was on fire with no sign of cooling off. His hand found her feminine center, which was still covered by the thong. He slid it to the side so he could play with her sex. Cole rubbed along the smooth hair of her apex. He twisted his fingers in it and enjoyed the feel along the tips of his fingers.

His hand continued until he felt her wetness. "Ummm, are you creaming for me, baby?"

"Yes" she whispered. "I want you to lick it up, baby. Take all of me; suck me dry with those big juicy lips of yours."

With her legs hanging over the edge of the bed, Cole buried his face in her femininity. The scent of her essence incited a riot of desire in him. He had to taste her. Cole did exactly as she'd begged, licking and tasting her wetness until she felt she would lose her mind. The feel of his tongue against her sensitive clit felt divine. When he squeezed her breasts with his hands, he slowly pushed her toward a climatic edge.

Kayla bucked against his mouth, and he drove his tongue deeper inside of her, in and out, until the first shudder of release was followed by an all out guttural scream of passion. Thrashing on the carefully made bed, Kayla tossed the pillows to the floor and held onto the covers for dear life as wave after wave of orgasm surged through her.

Yet, Cole was unrelenting. Without waiting for her to come down from her sexual high, he plunged his sheathed, hard penis deep into her succulent space.

"Oh yes, come on, baby, make me come again." Kayla raised her hips to receive every tantalizing inch of him, bucking wildly and loving the slap of his body against hers. "Pump me, baby, give it all to me."

"Like this?" Stroke… "Like this?" Stroke…longer…"Like this?" Stroke….even longer….

"Oh gawd yes," Kayla gasped in sweet agony as he teased her. "Oh gawd!"

Holding back the desire to dive deep into her wetness, for his own release, Cole teased her again with slow strokes until she begged for more. When he couldn't stand it another second, he gave her all of him. He pumped with reckless abandon, taking her to new heights of ecstasy. Sweat soaked body against body, they soared higher until they reached passion's peak in a blinding explosion of fiery sensation.

"Merciless," he said.

"Wicked."

"Damn, I love you."

"I love you more." *Hmmm*….she sighed. "Ready for round two?"

"I thought you'd never ask."

The following night's anniversary event was the program Cole and Robert had worked on for several weeks, and the source of Cole's many late nights in the office working on the questions and responses to the magazine's readers.

With Robert serving as the master of ceremonies, it was show time. "And now, please welcome to the stage, the editor and co-owner of *Full Flava Magazine*, Cole Lewis."

Wild applause filled the air of the auditorium. Robert made the announcement with the flair and style of an experienced MC.

Cole jogged onto the stage, feeling more exhilarated than he ever had before.

"Thank you, thank you. I can't tell you how much it means for me to come back to my alma mater to celebrate five years of a dream. *Full Flava* is the culmination of a lot of sleepless nights, lots of coffee and lots of support from people like you."

After a full minute of applause he continued, "Today's event is successful in part because of our sponsors and contributors. We can't go on without thanking them. Much love to USC for allowing me to come back, and to the readers who sent in letters to our advice columnists and to myself as editor. Some, I'll be sharing with you today. Some, I'm going to be calling your momma's…some of y'all taught this brotha new positions. You're just scandalous!" He waved his hands in mock surrender. "I'm just joking. Okay, thanks also to the company that provided the T-shirts and other promotional items, and last but certainly not least, my wonderful staff—my partner, Robert, administrative assistant, Cassandra and Ed in the mailroom. Because of their hard work, everyone here today will receive a complimentary copy of the magazine. The writers of the letters I read on stage will also receive a free one-year subscription to the magazine. And one lucky winner gets the keys to a brand new midnight blue BMW X5."

The announcement generated thunderous applause and whistles. Robert and Cassandra exchanged a look of *I have no idea what he's talking about.*

Happily watching from the side of the stage, Kayla was proud of the way her man worked the crowd. He was even more of a ham than she thought. Everyone was having a good time, and the refreshments she served from the diner were a big hit. Kayla looked skyward. *See Mom and*

Dad; we're doing good. A feeling of warmth and contentedness spreaded over her as she hugged her arms to her sides.

While he talked, the stagehands prepared the set for Cole so he could read a couple of letters. Kayla laughed along with the crowd as Cole put on a Hugh Hefner like robe and reading glasses and sat behind a desk.

The image was totally unlike his home office behavior. She licked her lips, just thinking about their last intimate encounter. *Ummm…*how they'd just recently *used* his office. The scene on stage conjured up pleasant images of being thoroughly loved atop his thick mahogany desk.

Cole cleared his throat in an exaggerated manner before he began. "Dear *Full Flava*,

I love your magazine, but can you add more spice? Crystal.

Dear Crystal, Thank you for your letter. I'm sending you a T-shirt, a copy of the magazine and some red hot pepper flakes."

The crowd applauded while they laughed.

Cole continued reading letters and playing up to the crowd.

Finally, he said, "Thank you all for coming out today. We have more giveaways, more music, more food and more magazines. Have a great time and join us for the gala tonight in the auditorium."

Someone from the crowd yelled, "What about the X5?"

"Oh, so you want my new car, huh?"

The stagehands came back out and changed the "set." This time a table with two chairs, a bottle of champagne, and candles were brought out. Again, Robert and Cassandra exchanged that look. Then the lights were lowered and the music came up. The crowd went crazy as Miles Jaye came to the stage playing his song "Irresistible."

Kayla watched, puzzled by this next transition, but she enjoyed the music like everyone else. Miles played a couple of his other popular songs then left the stage after a man hug from Cole.

Cassandra and Robert cheered wildly. Cassandra said, "Now that's a brotha in love. I didn't know boss man had it in him. Think any of that will rub off on you?"

Robert responded, "You never know what can happen when you play your cards right."

Smiling seductively, Cassandra said, "No, *you* play your cards right and see what happens." To punctuate her point, she stroked the inside of his thigh.

"Oh, a nasty girl. I like it."

"Pay attention. It looks like Cole isn't finished," she said as she grinned.

On stage, Cole continued to play to the crowd like a masterful musician himself. Finally, he sat down at the table and pulled out another letter. He motioned toward the side for Kayla to join him.

Her heart thumped triple time in her chest as she walked toward him. Cole helped her into the seat across from him, poured a glass of champagne, and then read the next letter.

"Dear Kayla Williams,

My sources at the magazine tell me that I have fallen deeply, madly and crazily in love with you. And considering the way you make me feel whenever you're around, I have to agree. Will you marry me? Sincerely, Cole Lewis, faithful editor-in-chief."

He moved from around the table to face her and knelt before her. Then he slid the diamond ring he held in his hands onto her ring finger.

Tears of joy streamed down Kayla's face. "Yes. Yes, you romantic, crazy man. I will marry you."

The crowd responded with more applause as Cole rose from bended knee and took her in his arms. Cole jangled the keys to his vehicle for all to see before he pressed them into Kayla's hand. The laughter and cheering continued. But all was forgotten once his lips made contact with hers.

The kiss was slow, languid, deep and passionate. *I'll take heaven for $200.00, Alex.* Kayla succumbed to the divine ecstasy of her lips against his. The intimate, heady feel of his body against hers sent heat spiraling in all directions. Cole deepened the kiss as his tongue continued its erotic exploration of her mouth and full lips. Kayla felt herself melt into his broad chest. They stood locked in a tender embrace on stage until time and space ceased to exist.

Miles Jaye played that sweet sax of his in the background until the curtain fell.

The celebration continued into the late hours of the evening. The chaste kisses they shared during the party filled them with eager anticipation for the passion to come at home.

David watched the scene, disgusted. A look of pure disdain marred his normally handsome features. He couldn't believe his eyes…they were acting like two hormonal teens instead of like grown folk. A bitter taste filled his mouth. Kayla and Cole had refused to heed his warnings. Didn't Kayla understand she was meant to be with him?

The world could be hers. He could give her everything. He was ambitious, talented, with the looks and charm to succeed. Her rejection of him was unthinkable.

The longer he watched, the more emotion welled up in him and threatened to spill over. Embarrassment turned to anger and anger to fury.

They'd made a fool of him with this public display of their commitment. The veins pulsed on the side of his neck. *I never lose.*

A new plan formed in his head as he drove away from the campus. *I never lose.*

CHAPTER FOURTEEN

The gala and awards banquet were as much a success as the earlier programs. The magazine was the talk of the town, but at the moment, there were two people who didn't care about anything but the magnetic pull each had to the other. Sensual excitement electrified the air as Kayla and Cole snuggled in each other's arms.

Tonight, they would make love tenderly and slowly. With her head on his chest, Kayla listened to the rhythmic beat of her lover's heart. She loved the sound as she lay next to him, the warm skin of his body matching the heat of her own. It was comfortable, satisfying and sensual. She replayed his proposal in her mind. A delighted grin spread across her face. It was such a crazily romantic thing for him to do. "How long had you been planning the proposal?"

"About nine months. I knew I wanted to marry you after that first catfish meal."

"Cole Lewis, you are so crazy."

"Damn right I am, crazy about you."

Kayla began to stroke Cole's muscular chest, she loved the creamy, light brown color gently bronzed to perfection. It reminded her of spiced butter—smooth and soft in all the right places. Her hand followed the plane of his silhouette up and down his chest to his abdomen then back again to his brown nipples. She squeezed gently at first then increased the pressure until she heard his breathing become faster and felt his heart pump faster against her ear. Down again, she slid her hand, this time she went past his six-pack abs. Kayla teased the hair surrounding his magnificent sex, which had sprung to life. Gently, she caressed him with her hands, from shaft to tip, tip to shaft, circling his head with the palm of her hand. Cole moaned in appreciation.

Inspired by his excitement, she wanted to give him more. Kayla moved to kiss his sweet lips. She let her hair, which had grown since their first meeting, cascade down the sides of her face onto his body. The feel of it as satin on his chest. Cole encircled her body with his arms, but she let him know that this was her show. He relaxed as he decided he would let her run things…for now.

Kayla crushed her lips to his, devouring their softness. As he opened for her, she explored his mouth with her tongue, searching, loving, and mating with him. After several erotic minutes, Kayla broke the kiss.

"You make me feel so damned good."

"That's the plan," she whispered.

She could feel his hard sex against her hips as she straddled him. Caressing him with her hands, she moved downward. His head pulsed underneath her, begging for attention. And she had no intention of disappointing.

Feather light touches along his length heightened his awareness of each movement. He stretched out and hardened with each brief moment of contact.

Her mouth replaced her hand and fingers. She enveloped his head in her warmth, teasing, tasting, and sucking him until she heard him moan with intensity. *Yeah, that's more like it.* In a natural response to the way she made him feel, Cole pumped his big penis in her mouth. She allowed him to dictate the pace for a bit, then took over again, taking him in as far as she could. But she needed more. "Baby, stand up for me."

"Baby, I'm too close, I don't know how much longer I can hold out."

She sucked hard, going down slow and coming up fast.

"Oh gawd, oh gawd." He surrendered to her seduction. "Dammit, woman, you win."

He moved off the bed to lean against the wall.

Kayla took her hand and squeezed his sac. A little cum oozed from his penis, which she immediately licked up as she took him back into her mouth. Reaching around for his firm buttocks, she brought him closer. In and out, in and slowly out, in slowly and out, she suckled him using her tongue and lightly her teeth to bring him to the edge of madness. Cole wrapped his fingers in her hair, making it a tangled mess.

"That's right baby, come for me, come for Mama." She plunged him deep into her warm, wet mouth digging her nails into the sensitive skin of his ass.

"Oh shit, baby, that feels too good." The battle for control was lost with one final long stroke. "Oh gawd, baby, I'm coming now!" *Ahhhhh.*

Panting for air and grateful for the wall, Cole leaned against it as his knees buckled.

Kayla kissed his wet cum covered sac before she went back to the bed. Her ass and breasts beckoned to him. Cole liked everything about her body.

Hot and ready for satisfaction herself, Kayla spread her legs wide for him. He stayed at the wall a little longer intrigued by what the little vixen would do next. She suckled two fingers, then circled each nipple springing both to life. She teased them with one hand, while she let the other slowly descend to her waiting sex. Her fingers dipped low, reveling in the juice, dripping from her spot.

Cole continued to watch as his breathing came back to normal. Kayla rubbed harder, increasing the pressure on her delicate clit until her eyes closed from the delicious swirl of warmth in her core. She lazily opened her eyes when she felt her lover's tongue replace the pressure of her fingers. Her muscles clenched around his long tongue as he ate her like she was his morning, noon, and night meal. Cole took it to the next level with his fingers. The combination of his expert tongue against her clit and his fingers inside her…

"Suck me, suck me baby." Heat, fire and explosions of light were all she felt. Cole gave her all he had. He sucked hard, until he felt the spasms of her climax course through her shaking body.

He held her gaze, this beautiful woman he wanted more than air. "I need to feel you baby."

Breathing in ragged gasps, she said, "Then what are you waiting for? Make me come again."

With no need for further encouragement, Cole put on a condom and rode the wave of her ecstasy. As he pumped into her, she raised her body to receive him. With her arms wrapped around him, she matched him thrust for wonderful thrust. Deeper and harder, she took everything he had to offer and gave it back.

He dipped his mouth to kiss her lips, already parted in passion. The kiss he delivered was fervently demanding, increasing the pleasure until she felt she couldn't handle anymore. Locked together until the fire built to capacity, the first shudders of release arced through her. Cole continued his sensual assault, bringing her higher and higher.

Without words he told her just how much he loved her. With one long, deep thrust, he entered her, staying there until her cries of passion matched his. Soaked...sated...and spent, they lay in each other's arms, enveloped by feelings of love. Their commitment to each other was eternal.

The next morning, her body still hummed from the night's activities. She stretched languidly in bed as she said, "That was some celebration, Mr. Lewis. I'll never doubt your ability to *surprise* again."

His dimpled smile warmed her heart. "I do what I can." He paused, then asked in a husky voice, "Kayla, are you happy?"

There were no words to describe how wonderful she felt. "Yes, I am. I have everything in the world any woman could ever want. I have the sexiest, most handsome, kind, talented, brilliant and gentle man." Kayla smiled. "I love you, Mr. Lewis."

"And I love you, future Mrs. Lewis." Cole waggled his eyebrows.

"I'm inclined to believe you do; however, I think I need empirical proof. Could you show me just how much?"

With her head leaned back into his embrace, she parted her lips for a kiss, which he gladly gave to her as he savored her sweetness. Cole whispered sweetly in her ear, "I think you may be a little overdressed for this demonstration."

Giggling, Kayla said, "You've been so brilliant since I've known you, and here you are right again."

All teasing stopped as Cole brought his lips to hers in a sensual, erotic kiss. His tongue found hers in a delicious duel for supremacy. Kayla met him stroke for stroke in power and intensity. Neither one willing to come up for air, neither one ready to give up.

The blood pounded through her veins to match the erratic beat of her heart. Before Cole, she'd never understood the concept of swooning, but once again, he took her to new heights. Between buckled knees and kisses to lightheadedness, Cole gave her new lessons in love.

But it wasn't just passion that made her pause. Kayla stiffened momentarily. Warning bells rang in her head as the short hairs on the back of her neck stood straight up. Tremors began at her toes and then spread up her entire body.

Alarmed by her reaction, Cole said, "Kayla, what is it sweetheart?"

"I'm not sure." Kayla shook her head, as if to banish unpleasant thoughts. "I just got this weird feeling."

"Isn't this just cozy?" David appeared from his hiding space in the closet where he'd been hiding all night, brandishing a large knife he had taken from Cole's kitchen.

Both sprang up from the bed and stared in shocked silence.

He clapped his hands in mock appreciation. "You two are quite the pair—too bad I didn't have my video or digital camera going; we might have made some money on Internet porn sites."

Cole instinctively moved in front of Kayla. "What the hell are you doing here?"

After a few awkward seconds, she found her voice then asked the same question, "Why are you acting like this? David, what are you doing here?" She hastily put on her robe while David's attention was turned to Cole.

The look of pure disdain he gave her was frightening. "Shut up and get over there next to *golden rod*."

Kayla moved back into Cole's arms. David snickered. "Did I say touch him, dammit. We're going to play a little game."

The knife shook in his hand. "What did I have to do, Kayla? I gave you every opportunity in the world to leave this loser and let me be the one for you. I had it all planned, darling. The wedding, the gown, the flowers and the honeymoon. You rejected it all for him."

He paused as the knife shook visibly from emotion. "I always thought you were the smart one in our relationship, but now I think I gave you too much credit."

Cole couldn't listen to this mad man anymore. Enough was enough. "David, what the hell do you want?" Cole wasn't about to let this lunatic get the upper hand.

Exhausted from being holed up in Cole's closet, David relaxed a little as he sat down on the edge of the bed.

"You call me a loser, yet I'm the one with Kayla, hmmm," Cole continued to throw David off balance.

David sprang up from the bed. "You're damn right, I'm the smart one. Smart enough to use your ex-girlfriend to get what I wanted. How do you think I got into your place?"

"This is insane, David. Just get out of here." Kayla glared at him, unable to believe what she was hearing. "Go on with your life like I have, before you lose everything. How do you think the bank is going to react to you being hauled off to jail for attempted assault?"

Incensed by her continual rejection, David raised his hand to strike her, but as he did, Cole seized the opportunity to take control of the situation. The blow he delivered knocked David to the floor, but like a cat, he sprung up again and managed to wrap his hands around Cole's throat.

Cole, the bigger of the two men, wrestled his hands away as he landed a solid punch to David's kidney area.

David kept coming until Cole threw a blow that knocked him out cold.

Kayla jumped off the bed to remove the knife before David couldn't grab it again. Together they bound David, dressed and then waited for the police to arrive.

Cole and Kayla were breathless over the struggle. In silence, they held each other tight…there were no words to describe their feelings.

Moments later, sirens and knocks on the door broke them apart. Detective Duncan was the first on the scene. "I guess now the police can do something!" she remarked to him.

After sorting out the mess and giving their statements, David was hauled off in a police car.

Alone in the room again, Cole took her in his arms. "Kayla, let's get out of here."

She breathed a sigh of relief. "Thank you. I don't think I could sleep here tonight."

They arrived at the Marriott Hilton Head Golf Resort, battle weary from their ordeal but thankful for their lives.

Once they were safely in their room, Kayla gave in to the pent up emotion she felt. Tears welled in Kayla's eyes. "I didn't know if we were going to make it. David was acting like such a damned maniac. Cole, I love you so much. Just hold me."

"Shush…we made it, darlin'. David didn't win; we did and we're just fine." Cole stroked her hair and shoulders while he held her.

A shudder passed through her. "I don't know what I would have done if anything happened to you. Cole, I know now you are my world."

"And you're mine. David will have a long time to think about his actions and I'm sure he'll never be able to hurt us again." He stroked the side of her face. "Let's forget all about the past and focus on the future."

After a shower together, they lay in bed with her head on his chest. In the silence, each tried to make sense of what had happened. Determined not to let David haunt her, she listened to Cole's heartbeat until the sound comforted her and her mind took her to a calm relaxed place.

Kayla decided they needed to make new memories to replace the bad. She stroked his bare chest, teasing each nipple to a hard bud. Then she swirled her long slim fingers through the light covering of hair that grew out of his chest, twisting and turning in erotic patterns.

Cole loved how she made him feel. He followed her lead and began to make sensual patterns of his own on her skin.

His lips found hers, and he kissed her insistently. He explored her mouth with his tongue and gently sucked hers, bringing forth quiet moans of pleasure.

After he protected them, he slipped into heaven. Cole stroked her with the patience of a practiced lover. He let her dictate the pace and depth, and then followed her lead. They made slow sensual love to each other until the name David Sutton ceased to exist.

Reveling in the sweet sensation he sent spiraling through her, Kayla found herself begging for more. She used words she hadn't even known were in her vocabulary. If he made her feel any better, she would be speaking in tongues.

Thrust for wonderful thrust, they took each other to the precipice, ready to fall into the marvelous wonder of orgasm. She screamed out his name at the same time that he called out hers. Their mutual climax was powerful…explosive…blinding.

"I love you, Kayla."

"I love you too, Cole."

She smiled up at her husband-to-be. "Maybe the next time we come back to this hotel, it will be to the honeymoon suite."

A sexy smile crept along his full lips, as he said, "I'll make the reservation now."

EPILOGUE

One year later…

Kayla laughed hysterically. "Cole, be careful, you're going to drop me."

"If you don't stop moving around so much I will."

They tumbled over the threshold into the newly completed restaurant with Cole wiping sweat from his brow. "You know, you don't have to direct and orchestrate everything. I got this."

Kayla lifted the train of her white designer wedding gown. "I know I don't," she teased, "but it's so much fun."

"Come here, woman. My incorrigible vixen." He took her in his arms and kissed her soundly.

"Hey, hey, save that for later, you've got company!" Tracey boomed from the entryway where the guests had gathered to await the couple's arrival. The rest of their wedding guests whooped and cheered.

Cole took Kayla into his arms again. This time the kiss was deeper and longer. Kayla's knees buckled under the pressure.

The loud pop of a champagne cork finally broke the two apart. Tracey teased as she steered her toward the head table. "This is the reception, not the honeymoon."

"Yes, ma'am." With a sigh, Kayla looked toward her groom. "I guess we have to be sociable. But tonight, you're all mine."

Cole slowed their movement toward the table to whisper in her ear. His deep bass voice filled their intimate space. "I'm all yours *every* night."

Happily, she twisted the little band of gold sitting behind her 2-carat diamond solitaire. "Yes, you are."

Dangerous Dilemmas

The music began to play as Kayla and Cole turned their attention from each other back to their guests. They thanked their guests for coming to celebrate their special day.

The new Lewis family had a lot to celebrate with the grand opening of the new *KW's Bar and Grille* the completion of their waterfront dream home, and the overwhelming success of the magazine.

There was only one thing to make her life absolutely perfect. And if all went well tonight, it would occur in about nine months. Kayla smiled mischievously.

Just then, Cole turned toward her. Desire sizzled between them from mere eye contact. This time she skirted his embrace before he could take her in his arms again. She wanted him to save some of that enthusiasm for their honeymoon suite.

Smiling, Kayla announced, "Okay, everyone, it's time for the garter belt and bouquet toss. All you eager and not so eager singles gather around." She looked pointedly at Tracey, who winked in response.

After she was in position with one long leg on a chair, Cole knelt down on one knee to remove her garter belt. Kayla had made it a point to place it high up around her thigh.

A challenge Cole eagerly accepted as he removed it with excruciating slowness. He took his time while he made feather touches with his fingertips all the way down the creamy, soft skin of her inner thigh. By the time he was finished stroking every inch, Kayla wanted to clear the restaurant's hall. For his ears only, she said, "Oh, Mr. Lewis, how you will pay for this. Just wait until tonight."

He smiled up at his new bride. "Promises, promises."

Parker Publishing, LLC

Group Discussion Questions:

1. Do you think we have any control over whom we fall in love with?

2. Do you think it was selfish of Kayla to want to change the restaurant to a bistro?

3. Do you think Kayla had unreasonable control issues?

4. Did Cole give in to Kayla too much?

5. What could Kayla have done differently with Cole?

6. Do you think Sheila should have faced criminal charges?

7. Do you think Sheila loved Cole too?

8. Should we have stronger stalker laws in the country?

9. Do you think Kayla and Cole had sex too early?

10. Do you think Kayla and Cole made a good couple and will be happy?

11. Do you believe that we can communicate with the dead?

About the Author

Katherine D. Jones, author of the Special Corruption Unit series, is a multi-published author with several magazine articles, short stories and books in print. Katherine regularly writes for nationally distributed magazines, *Black Romance*, *Bronze Thrills* and *True Confessions*.

Her SCU series consists of the novels, *Love Worth Fighting For* and *Worth the Wait*, both published by BET Arabesque Books; *Undercover Lover* and the final book in the SCU series, *Deep Down*, published by Kensington Dafina romance.

Her third novel, *Undercover Lover* was recently recognized in *Essence Magazine* as suggested reading for Valentine's Day 2006.

Katherine's novella, "Gunns and Roses," appeared in the Parker Publishing anthology, *Cuffed by Candlelight*, released in February 2007. This, her second Parker Publishing release, *Dangerous Dilemmas* takes erotic suspense to an exciting new level.

Katherine describes her writing as contemporary romance fiction with a twist, because she likes to give her readers an unexpected ride.